The Pact

"…JoAnn Fastoff has written a novel that you will find yourself unable to put down in her latest continuation of the Howard Watson Intrigue series."

Paige Lovitt
for Reader Views (2008)

"Fastoff gives an authentic view of criminal investigation with a touch of believable technology…(The Pact) is a thriller of a story!"

Det. George Patton (retired)
Chicago Police Dept/FBI Chicago
Violent Crimes Task Force

"Wow! All I can say is (Fastoff) never lets me down when it comes to action that I can visualize."

Elliott V. Porter
Chicago Filmmaker and Actor

The Gordian Knot

"A fast-paced and suspenseful novel, enjoyable for diverse readership…"

Reader Views Shelf

"I thought I was a seasoned mystery reader. Fastoff has proven me wrong. She put a twist, or was it a turn…that delightfully surprised me."

Sam Rodgers – Utter Hip Magazine

THE
Lie

JoAnn Fastoff

authorHOUSE®

AuthorHouse™
1663 Liberty Drive
Bloomington, IN 47403
www.authorhouse.com
Phone: 1-800-839-8640

Published by AuthorHouse   3/13/2012

ISBN: 978-1-4685-5694-0 (sc)
ISBN: 978-1-4685-5695-7 (e)

Library of Congress Control Number: 2012903490

Acknowledgements

As always, my writing is dedicated to my offspring Angela and David, and my goddaughter Angelita. To my main squeeze – Ron Damasauskas, who read and re-read this "like a man" – thanks... seriously! Once again to the "editing bookends" – my sisters Rebecca and Carol thank you, 'cause I know this hurt. To my consultant and friend, Vaughn Taylor Akutagawa for imparting his clever "Cliff Notes Japanese". To Dr. Lane Ashmore, thanks for investing in me; after 48 years we're still best friends! To Ken Webb, one of the best private eyes I know – thanks for your insight. To Randy Richardson, President of Chicago Writers Association – you are the best! To Paige Lovitt at Reader Views, what can I say? You have been so kind in reviewing my work for the past seven years that I must follow through and finally meet you! To Mitch Butler who taught me about world view, thanks so much for listening to me ad nauseam. To Julius Artwell at AuthorHouse who kept his word – thank you!

Lastly, to my mom Sarah who lives vicariously through me and is indeed the better writer – I love you.

Thank you God for Howard Watson.

JAF

1991

Kabinda, a village located in the south central Democratic Republic of the Congo - a country in central Africa.

As the rock-laden cart carried him and the four men to the surface of the volcanic crater, Peter Samadu was finally able to feel the sun's rays. He could also feel the scowl on the mercenaries' faces that were waiting for them with AK-47 assault rifles. Peter and the men had been down in the crater for more than ten hours. No extra water or food was provided - only what was given 10 hours prior. As soon as he and the men jumped off the cart, they started coughing from the sudden burst of clean air that hit their lungs. Their bounty, in this case, the cart that held the kimberlite rocks, was wheeled away from them. They could go home now.

Peter headed for the path that led down the mountain slope. Three miles later, he could hear the rush of the Bushimaie River and the smells that signaled home. A lean-to stood on a wedge of land in which *The Company* said his family could live. He shared this shanty with his parents, five sisters and brothers. The wedge of land had belonged to his family 130 years before *The Company* came.

Peter's mother waved to him as he came into sight. He picked up his pace until his 12-year old heart told him he would not make it.

He then thanked God for his time on earth.

\#

Lie = **meant to deceive.**

PART 1

Six years later - Philadelphia, PA

The man ran faster, slowing only to see if the four thugs were still chasing him. He held tight to the briefcase as he raced down a darkened street. The Ben Franklin Bridge loomed high above his head. *Why did I come this way? Even if they get the briefcase, they can't open it without the keys.* He continued running. He looked behind him again and noticed the men had disappeared. He breathed a sigh of relief. As he turned the corner, the men were waiting for him. "Trust me," he pleaded, "this briefcase will only bring you a lot of trouble. You have no idea who it belongs to; take my money and my wallet but leave the briefcase with me."

The four laughed and circled the man. One thug took a thick chain from his jacket pocket and started swinging it around his head. They closed in on the man and the last thing he said was "I'm sorry Joop".

#

Chapter 2

Washington, D.C.

Howard Watson had just pulled into his parking space at the J. Edgar Hoover FBI Building when he noticed his Bureau Section Chief, Alberto Marino, motioning to him from the steps of the building. He found this to be uncharacteristic of Marino who was rarely demonstrative. His demeanor seemed to suggest that he had been waiting for Howard for a while. *Why didn't he just call me on my cell?* Howard subsequently reached in his jacket and felt for the phone he then recalled leaving on the kitchen counter? "Damn!" he yelled.

When Howard reached the steps of the massive building, he took a deep breath and soaked in Marino's lashing.

"Howard" Marino began. "I've been trying to get you on your cell for the past hour". Before he could continue the lecture, Howard apologized for the mix-up. "Sorry Al, I inadvertently left my phone on the counter in the kitchen; kill me if you must." With that, he hung his head like a man on his way to the gallows.

Marino would normally have found this scene amusing mainly because Howard was not one to lose things, or forget things.

However, not today.

"What's up with you lately?" he asked.

"You don't want to know" Howard answered.

"Yeah...I do" Marino shot back.

"Okay. George is playing soccer. Lawrence is into baseball. Mark is home from law school. Carol got a taste of courtroom drama and now wants to litigate again. My parents are here for a week. Want more?"

Marino got his answer.

Marino was thinking that it was not like Howard to buckle under seemingly minor problems. But then again he had known Howard for 22 years and remembered when he wasn't married, when he wasn't a father, when he wasn't aware he wasn't happy, when he was just a shell of a person. Listening to Howard now made Marino conclude that this was a complete man, problems and all.

Nevertheless, business was at hand.

"I want you to gather your troops, specifically Yamamoto, and head to Philadelphia to assist their office in helping the local P.D. on a couple of murders that might interest you."

Howard's curiosity was piqued. "What's up?"

Marino took a moment before answering perhaps the best Supervising Agent he had on board. "A gang called the Pit Bulls has been wreaking havoc, extortion-wise, among diamond dealers. A couple of weeks ago a man's body was found with chain link around his neck near Philly's diamond district. He was carrying a letter in the breast pocket of his suit that read that if his body was found, a briefcase was missing. Well, the "briefcase" was missing. I want you and Yamamoto to see what's up, and find out about this missing briefcase."

"Is there something you're not saying Al? How come Philly can't take care of this?"

"They can Howard; Philly Bureau requested *your* expertise as Lead Agent because the Pit Bulls deal in guns, which is right up your alley."

He took a pause.

"Howard?"

"Yeah Al?"

"You know the main Pit Bull. He's from Moscow; goes by the name of Krakevich."

"Ptor Krakevich?"

"Same guy."

"I thought he died. I read you the California Office Notification about five years ago that said Krakevich was found dead in some beach house fire in I believe, LaJolla, and that he was positively identified through dental records."

"Yeah well, DNA now says the dental records positively belonged to someone else. Maybe even Stalin."

Howard chuckled. "So Krakevich is alive huh? Damn. What else?"

"Philadelphia Bureau doesn't have a Russian expert and they believe Krakevich, who now goes by the name of Nikola Gregorvsky is probably behind this rash of jewelry pillaging. The gem community is afraid, believing they have no recourse but to buckle under these hoodlums. They're also of the opinion that some in the Philadelphia P.D. are working for these Russians; the money is that good. If these jewelers leave Philadelphia, big money goes with them. The city can't afford to let this industry move elsewhere because they bring in a lot of customers, consequently bringing in a lot of money for the city."

"Do we have any idea as to the contents of the briefcase?"

"No. Whatever is in the briefcase is more than likely not

good news. Whoever took the briefcase has no idea the level of information it might contain."

Marino glanced at a black limousine pulling up. "I'm on my way to a meeting but I want to meet with you and Yamamoto this afternoon - say around 2pm. In the meantime, find out all you can about "Lazarus" Krakevich. I do not think whoever killed that person in Philly was out to rifle some unsuspecting man walking down a street with a briefcase. The perpetrator knew him, or knew of him. The person or persons behind this also knew to take the briefcase."

The black limo stopped at the bottom of the stairs. Marino leaned into Howard. "I'll talk to you later."

Howard watched Marino slide into the backseat of the vehicle. He was wondering who else was in the car. When the limo drove off, he strolled into the FBI building and toward his office.

#

Chapter 3

Carol Watson was trying her best to accommodate her twin sons in their quest for sports transportation to separate parts of the Virginia geography. Her oldest son, Mark, had just finished his first year of law school and was trying to dodge her but got caught in the undertow. "Mark!" she called, "It would mean so much to me if you could take George to his soccer game and Lawrence to his baseball game. I'm taking your grandparents to the mall so I just can't handle your brothers right now."

Mark glanced over at his beautiful, talented mother and hung his head. He was thinking that if he did not love her so much he would just as soon drop the twin knuckleheads into the Potomac. However, the only answer that escaped his lips was "Okay Mom, you got it. Do I have to pick them up? I mean aren't they old enough to take a bus home?"

Carol could only shake her head. "Please find it in your busy schedule of nothing to pick them up too, okay?" Although she knew Mark would be working in a law library in a week, she thought it best to arm him with as much to do until then.

Mark half-nodded and called the two knuckleheads, who immediately started running, dropping gear everywhere, and headed toward the SUV, parked in the driveway. All three sons waved to their mom and then they were gone.

Carol watched the vehicle until it was no longer in sight. She was so happy that all three offspring were home for the summer. Despite her "nagging", George and Lawrence had developed into real people over the past year. They even chose not to go away to camp thinking it "too babyish" and subsequently joined summer sports teams. The thought then hit her hard - *wasn't it only yesterday that Mark was holding his twin brothers in his arms? Has eleven years really passed? Where did the time go?*

She closed the door and tried not to think about it.

#

Chapter 4

Kelly Yamamoto was excited but at the same time uneasy about the news - she was pregnant. "Oh my God!" she said to her doctor. "What if Tim isn't happy? What if he's disappointed? What if he doesn't want a baby?"

Dr. Alcott smiled; "typical new mother" she thought.

Kelly was thinking differently. She and Tim had been married for over 10 years and she really wanted children. Dr. Alcott had mentioned to her that because of her age she would have to be very careful in her pregnancy. Kelly heard her say things like "amniocentesis", "miscarriage", and even "Down Syndrome". She tried not to listen but she was in the medical field; she was a scientist. She knew the dangers associated with a first time mother giving birth in her late 30's. However, that wasn't what concerned her most. What concerned her most was the response she would get from Tim, who was now comfortable with the DINK moniker: "double income, no kids". *How will I tell him?*

\#

Chapter 5

Janet J. Forrestal had been with the Philadelphia FBI office for almost three years before she went on an actual stakeout. Prior to that, her job had been mostly limited in scope, like sitting at the front desk taking walk-in complaints, or appearing at job fairs and college recruitment events. Now she was going into the field with other agents – show time! She proved her mettle quickly by assisting in the captures of a pedophile that had been on the lam for six years, and a serial rapist specializing in prostitutes in Philadelphia's central city area.

Although she never divulged her secret, Janet had wanted to be an FBI agent ever since she was a kid. She did not know one single woman agent prior to her appointment, but she quickly got to know the eight women agents stationed in the New York and Philadelphia bureaus. The reason? The FBI's new public relations campaign was trying to illustrate how diverse the FBI had become. Janet would just shake her head at this exhaustive and expensive exercise. It was not as if she wouldn't be noticed. She was 5'10" tall, red haired, and owned damn near every freckle east of the Mississippi River. On top of that, she was Black.

Yep, she thought, I have finally made it into the big leagues. *Why are Headquarters sending agents to Philadelphia to "assist" with a case that my partner and I are close to getting a handle on? Something is up.*

Headquarters had notified the Philadelphia Bureau that Janet and her partner needed more leads and more labor. Okay, maybe she agreed with needing more leads. There were no fingerprints found on the chain link around this victim's neck, nor the three other victims found in the last 15 months. (There were no fingerprints found on the same type of note left neither in this victim's breast pocket nor with the three other victims.) Finally, yet most importantly, there were no witnesses. *Not yet.*

This last victim looked vaguely familiar for some odd reason but Janet couldn't place him. His name, Harry Dennis, didn't ring a bell either. However, he disturbed her. Her partner, Gil Holloway, made his usual crude remark, "Maybe all white men are starting to look alike to you. Hahaha!" She thought it unfunny then…and now. However, he wasn't getting rid of her this easy. No matter how diverse the new FBI had become, it still fell short of the finish line in terms of equality for women. Even the Black and Latino male agents felt less than love for the women agents. *Go figure.*

Janet, to her surprise, found out just why the FBI had started aggressively recruiting women: "Women approach intellectual problems differently than men," the recruiter told her. "Women rely on the use of landmarks and are better able to remember whether items in a sequence had changed places". *Best-of-all?*

"Women's verbal skills, including verbal memory and fluency, are superior to men's. Women are excellent communicators and listeners. *You guys* are often able to gain trust to defuse and de-escalate potentially violent situations."

Yeah, yeah, yeah.

The FBI, she had been told "had enough qualified door kickers, so what were really needed were more agents who had the skills to *talk* a subject out of a barricaded room, removing the need to kick down a door in the first place."

None of this meant shit to most of the male agents who continued to believe the women were getting special privileges, like working soft assignments, or taking time off for having children. The FBI was still a male-dominated organization, but Janet didn't care, she'd heard all this before. Her mother hated the idea of her going into the FBI. Her father was on her mother's side. One of her two brothers asked if she was gay. So the idea of some male agent hating her for being there didn't even register. *As if!*

#

1979

Janet Forrestal graduated in the top one percent of her high school class in Philadelphia. Four years later, she graduated cum laude from Princeton University with a major in economics. In addition, she was fluent in Japanese. Even before graduation several major companies, one of which was an international banking conglomerate headquartered in Philadelphia, recruited her. Since she wanted to be close to home, she jumped at the opportunity with the bankers and started racking up awards and recognition immediately.

After a year of working for what seemed like forever on mundane projects, Janet was ecstatic at the request made to her by an Executive VP of the company to assist the

Philadelphia FBI office with an actual case. During the five months she was loaned to the Bureau, she was so impressed with the professionalism displayed by the Agents that she decided to go for it and apply to the Bureau.

Janet never really believed she would get into the Academy but *then stranger than strange happened.*

Her father was acquainted with the U.S. Senator from Pennsylvania who subsequently wrote a very compelling letter to the FBI detailing Janet's accomplishments academically as well as athletically and ethically. A year later her secret dream came true, she was an FBI Agent!

"Janet Juliana Forrestal!"

Although she heard her name, Janet was still in shock that she had actually gotten through FBI training and was now an FBI Agent. She glanced over at her father and then her mother who managed a weak, but genuine smile. Janet chuckled, as she knew her mother was proud of her accomplishment but not her career path. She also took a momentary glance at her two younger brothers who were giving her the "thumbs up" sign. She laughed. Yep, she was an agent, an FBI Agent! *Wow!* She crossed the stage, cheesed with the Bureau Section Chief, and smiled quickly at her partner Tim, who was on his way to the stage. She headed toward the holding room where the new agents had been herded. *Wow! An FBI Agent! Was it only 16 weeks ago that I had entered the class of training, training, and more training?*

Time does fly when you're having fun she thought. As she looked back at the FBI Training Academy, she remembered four months of grueling, punishing and demanding exercises and classroom training that made Princeton look elementary.

#

The screeching from the several Philadelphia patrol car radios and her partner brought her back to the present and to the body lying on the ground.

"How long are you going to stare at it?" Holloway asked loudly. *He has such a wonderful bedside manner.* Janet was thinking that it was damn near shocking to learn that he was single.

#

Chapter 6

Koriuko Hasai moved his family from Japan to the U.S. during the late 1950's. They settled in Philadelphia where he worked as an accountant for a small appliance manufacturing company. Five years later Koriuko became the owner of the business after his employers were gunned down in the company's parking lot. When no legal resident family member stepped forward to claim the business, Koriuko claimed *he* was a family member. The Small Business Administration officer stamped "license approved" on Koriuko's papers even though Koriuko looked Japanese and the family members had been Italian. The government officer didn't care; Koriuko was just another signature, and as long as the fee was paid and the owner stayed out of legal trouble, his job was done.

Two years after Koriuko's oldest son, Ichiro, graduated from Wharton with an MBA he became his father's partner. He added stainless steel manufacturing to the company's roster and by 1980, "Hasai Manufacturing Company" was operating in several locations. By 1995, the Hasai's owned 10 plants in Pennsylvania, New Jersey, and New York.

#

Chapter 7

Howard and Tim slowly trudged through FBI Bureau Section Chief Alberto Marino's oak doors. Both men had family obligations that made it impossible for them to be happy about a new assignment that took them out of their local geography. Howard could have easily given the forensic assignment to another agent, but because Tim was requested just as he was, he thought it best to keep the peace.

Carol is going to be mad. She had planned a little getaway for just the two of them and Howard's parents had even agreed to stay a week longer to make sure the twins didn't burn down the house while they were away. Unfortunately, they couldn't count on Mark because the last time he watched his two younger siblings it turned into a fiasco. Howard remembered the incident like it was yesterday:

He and Carol were returning from a fundraiser around midnight and after turning into their cul-de-sac, they could see from a distance their 15-year-old son Mark playing basketball in the driveway with his three-year-old brothers - at midnight! Carol was steamed.

\#

Tim had learned Kelly was pregnant. He hadn't told Howard yet because he didn't quite know how he felt. Kelly, on the other hand, was excited beyond belief. She had called her and Tim's parents before he could even state whether or not he wanted her to have this baby. Although he believed his marriage was good, it wasn't as solid as it had once been. He really felt children might rock the boat. *Damn! What am I going to do? What am I going to say to her?*

\#

"Good to see you both made it on time," Marino said with a smirk.

Howard and Tim planted themselves on Marino's plush chocolate leather sofa while Marino remained at his desk facing them. "Men, Philadelphia P.D. are experiencing a rash of jewelry hijackings that has left four men dead in the past 22 months. No fingerprints, no sign of any struggle, no...nothing. They're baffled. Philly Bureau hasn't come up with any concrete explanations either. Tim, I spoke with Howard this morning to explain why he was requested to work with Philadelphia - his Russian fluency. You were requested because of your forensic expertise. If it's okay with you Howard, I'd like someone from Tim's forensic team to accompany him.

"Sure Al", Howard answered while looking at Tim. "Can Ahmad Waverly be spared?"

"Yeah Howard", Tim answered. "I can move around some cases; no problem."

"I'm curious as to why Philly Bureau isn't using their own forensics team?" Howard asked Marino. "They're a crack operation; even Tim has mentioned it on several occasions." He then shot Tim a look of "go with me on this". Tim took his cue.

"Yes Chief, what can I teach *them*? It's not like they aren't always throwing their awards in our faces."

"Philadelphia P.D. believes there are dirty cops involved in this undertaking. The Bureau believes it too. Until the rotten apples can be fleshed out, Philly office needs your assistance on this. Both of you will be working with two agents: Gil Holloway, and Janet Forrestal. Tim, I believe you're acquainted with Forrestal...correct?"

"Yes chief," Tim said with a smile.

"Well, she and Holloway are itching to figure this one out. I just want you two to help them scratch that feeling. They're getting nowhere fast and the Philly jewelers want answers yesterday. In addition, I hope both of you recognize that working with a woman agent is the same as working with a man. An agent is an agent."

Howard smirked at Marino.

"Stan Abrams from the Philadelphia Office will meet us in the morning for a 10:00a.m. meeting. I want Waverly here too."

Marino paused. "That's about it unless you two have questions?"

"No? Good, see you later."

The agents were getting up to leave when Marino decided he had one more thing to say. "Tim, you're going to need your Japanese."

Tim started to ask Marino for more information but he just didn't want any more anything on his mind at this time. "You got it" is all that escaped his lips.

#

Chapter 8

Ahmad Waverly was pumped. He had been with the FBI for over 10 years and this was the very first time he had been requested to travel *to* a case. *It must be something extremely important.* He was ready for some excitement. Ten years earlier he had assisted in identifying the body parts of a so-called disgruntled army retiree named Carl Sunderland, who, with a former colleague of Ahmad's - John Mason, exposed upper level government misbehavior. The sting sent two U.S. senators and more than a few CIA agents to prison. In a later case, his contributions in figuring out a DNA sample led to the capture of serial killer Samuel Jacob Thorne in New York. Just the previous year he aided in a major drug bust in Chicago that resulted in two Russian heavies being deported and subsequently being sentenced to a labor camp for an indefinite amount of time.

Yep, my resume is sweet.

Now his boss, Tim Yamamoto, requested his presence at a meeting that included Howard Watson, Chief Marino and a Philadelphia SAC to discuss going to Philadelphia and assisting agents with a global problem: conflict diamonds. Waverly was pumped.

#

Chapter 9

Stanton Abrams, the Philadelphia Bureau Supervising Agent in Charge (SAC), was already seated in Marino's office when Waverly arrived ten minutes early. Marino had just started introductions when Tim Yamamoto and Howard Watson breezed through the doors. Whew! Waverly was happy to see them both. Once the additional babble of "welcome to D.C." etc. had died down, Abrams painted the scenario.

"Chief, Agents, about 22 months ago the first of four couriers was murdered in the Diamond District and left with chain link around his neck. Same type of murder for the next three couriers, same note left in the pocket...or placed in the pocket, we're not sure which, and a briefcase, according to the note, was always missing. These couriers, we believe, were carrying instructions in their briefcase describing where to purchase guns: automatics, assault rifles, carbines, shotguns...you name it. *For what you might ask*? To sell to various African, South American, and Russian factions staging military coups."

"According to the Philly M-E's report on the first victim,

lodged in his stomach were three of the finest, quality diamonds he had ever seen. They were so brilliant that the M-E had to call in a diamond expert to make sure they were authentic. The expert said that they were real. The second and third victims – same scenario: diamonds in the abdomen again. This last victim? He had two keys in his stomach - two keys."

Howard glanced quizzically at Marino for a moment.

Abrams continued. "This last victim, Harry Dennis, used to be an Agent in the '70s and '80s but got caught up in his own espionage bullshit and was sent to prison for about eight years. When he got out, I'm almost sure it was in '92..."

Marino nodded in agreement.

"...he pretty much disappeared. He had aged a lot so I *almost* didn't recognize him on the slab last week. It was depressing. Anyway, we need to know what Harry was doing with two keys in his belly and why he suffered the same fate as the other three departed souls. By the way, only a few of us know Harry was the body on the slab. At-this-time, we'd like to keep it that way."

Marino spoke. "So what's our contribution?"

"I'd like your permission for Agent Watson to lead my team in Philadelphia, especially with his Russian knowledge. I know this sounds as if I'm being vague, but this is all we know at this time. Our two agents assigned to this case, Holloway and Forrestal, haven't been able to penetrate any major cells yet but they can assist you with what they know at this time. In addition, Agent Yamamoto, your Japanese will come in handy with Forrestal's, as a certain American manufacturing giant also owns a Congolese rough diamond-trading firm. We want to make sure that his substantial operating capital comes from his manufacturing plants." He turned and looked at Howard. "The DEA and ATF will meet with us once you and your team hit town. We're hoping you can get your end together...perhaps by Thursday?"

"Right now, we have four bodies that can't let us in on their story. We need a story."

#

Chapter 10

Ptor Krakevich hailed from Moscow. In the 1930s, Josef Stalin exerted total control over all dissenters but especially writers, intellectuals, artists, musicians and scientists, and subjected them to forced obedience. Krakevich's only brother, Andrei, an intellectual, was not fully submissive to Stalin's rules and consequently perished during the terror wave of the late 1930s. Krakevich's longtime friend was Yuri Rostovsky. Both attended University together and both had become scientists despite the political ramifications. The death of Communism left them without jobs and made both men rely on the free enterprise system (steal low, sell high) forcing them to make a move to the United States.

Krakevich had learned too late that Rostovsky had been trapped in a FBI sting and subsequently extradited. Krakevich mentioned to Rostovsky on several instances to stay clear of the Peruvian Hector Cruz but Rostovsky did not heed his warning. Krakevich was quite saddened by the news of Rostovsky's travel back to Russia, as he knew first-hand there was no escape from a Russian work camp and that Rostovsky might die before ever getting out. *But to not become the target myself,* Krakevich decided he had to "die" in a fire. *I will not join my friend's fate in Siberia. In addition, I will not succumb to arrogance. I am now Nikola Gregorvsky.*

Howard was basking in the glow of his latest case – putting Rojelio Poniente, Peru's ersatz drug lord, behind bars for a long, long, time. He'd heard Poniente had already amassed an army in prison. *Good for him.* Now though, Howard was busy focusing on another roach: Nikola Gregorvsky.

#

Chapter 11

"I thought we were going to spend some time together?" was all Carol could deliver before she ran to the bedroom.

Howard shook his head and walked toward the room that was calling his name - in this case, the guest bedroom. He absolutely wanted to talk to her but he just didn't have the energy...not tonight. In the morning, he would deal with it...but not tonight.

Across the Potomac Tim was dealing with the same type of domestic battery. "Honey" he breathed deeply, "I'm just not sure of my feelings yet. Give me a moment to let this sink in."

Kelly looked at him as if he was the enemy. "What are you saying Tim, that you don't want this baby?"

"No, I'm not saying that Kell, I'm..."

She cut him off.

"Look Tim, I've had enough of us living our life *your* way with *your* rules and *your* rituals. When do we actually allow *me* some say in this marriage? Is this possible or..."

She couldn't finish the sentence, instead ran to the guest bedroom and slammed and locked the door. Tim heard her crying. He then looked up to the sky and thanked Buddha, Siddhartha, Jesus, Muhammad, and Moses for granting him breathing space for at least a week to work on the upcoming case in Philadelphia. *Perhaps by that time I will get up enough nerve to tell her the truth.*

#

Chapter 12

Howard, Tim, and Ahmad Waverly arrived at Philadelphia International Airport to throngs of picketing union workers. Plowing through the strikers in order to get to their waiting limo seemed to take almost as long as the flight from D.C. to Philly. Howard found himself thinking that the city workers in Philadelphia were always striking about something. *The City of Brotherly Love. Yeah, right.*

Although Stanton Abrams was in charge of assembling the various agencies that would make up the forthcoming task force, Bruce Jergensen was the Agent assigned to meet them. Jergensen was the Lead Alcohol, Tobacco, Firearms and Explosives Agency officer. He was looking forward to working with his friend Howard Watson again. "Welcome to Philadelphia!" he shouted. When the car was safely out of the airport, Jergensen handed a packet to all three men.

"Howard, it's good to see you!" he said while vigorously shaking Howard's hand. "What's it been - five, six years?"

"Six", Howard said with a grin. Both agents smiled at each other as if they knew a whole lot of something together but neither was going to tell. Tim studied both smiles. He would get Howard to spill the beans later, perhaps on the plane trip home.

Later in the afternoon Howard, Tim and Waverly, were ushered into a conference room at FBI Philadelphia Headquarters. Four agents from the Drug Enforcement Agency were already seated at the table. Bruce Jergensen and two of his agents from Alcohol, Tobacco, Firearms, and Explosives joined them, as did three Philadelphia FBI Agents: Stanton Abrams, Gilbert Holloway and Janet Forrestal.

Janet and Tim's eyes found each other. A smile crept over both faces, enough so that Howard noticed.

Stanton Abrams brought the assemblage to attention. "Agents" he began, "I want to thank you all for your participation. I especially want to thank Special Agents Jergensen and Watson for sharing Lead Agent in Charge of this task force."

His smile quickly faded. "Let's get down to business. All of you were given a packet regarding conflict, or as they say on the street "war" diamonds. I want to be adamant in insisting that you read the info completely as we will go over our strategy tomorrow morning. This mission will require all our attention as the conflict diamond war is out of control."

"For those of you not fully aware, the insurgents use diamonds and drugs to purchase ammunition and weapons to finance conflict. If this isn't bad enough they commit atrocious abuses to children by drugging and forcing them into their military."

"Our first assignment is to stay out of the politics. Our second assignment is to find the beginning of the chain that employs the couriers who deliver these bloodstones to the U.S. Our third assignment is to get rid of the chain."

"The second and third undertakings will require team

work from all your agencies. Because the courier crimes took place here in Philadelphia, we will start with the Philadelphia P.D. However, we divulge nothing more than necessary. Is everyone clear on this last message?"

Agents were clear on Abrams' message – tell Philadelphia P.D. only the obvious and work around them. When the meeting ended, Forrestal and Yamamoto quickly connected. Tim wasted no time in the introductions.

"Howard, Ahmad, I want you both to meet an academy buddy of mine, Janet Forrestal. Janet, this is my Supervising Lead Agent Howard Watson, and my top inventive guru Ahmad Waverly."

Forrestal reciprocated. "Agents Watson, Yamamoto and Waverly, I want you to meet my partner for the past two years, Gil Holloway."

Bruce Jergensen quickly introduced his team; the DEA followed suit. After the introductions died down the dozen or so agents immediately realized they had never assisted on a task force of this magnitude. The charge of electricity in the air was exciting but at the same time threatening. A nasty thought ran across Howard's mind: *these kinds of credentials in one place could only mean that someone on this assignment will not live to discuss the ending.*

#

"How have you been?" was all Janet could ask once they had some quiet time alone.

"I've been great" Tim answered. "You still speak our language?"

Janet smiled. "Konnichi wa?" she asked dryly, adding "Genki desu?" Tim cracked a large smile. "Konban wa" he fired back. For the next fifteen minutes, they spewed out the details of their lives speaking in Nihongo, the language of Japan.

#

1984

Carolyn Jessup and Janet Forrestal had been steered together as partners in the FBI Academy. Most of the men didn't want a woman partner, especially in the physical portion of the training. Okay, if they got a woman partner once they were in the field, so be it, but in the Academy where each trainee had to be the best physically, most of the men were comforted by the fact that there were *two* women trainees who could be partners.

Unfortunately, Jessup petered out in the fourth week and a collective gulp occurred among the men recruits. Most of them were relieved by the fact that of the two women who made the cut at least it was Janet as she could outrun, outshoot, and outmaneuver a few of them. Yep, she was in!

The male partner assigned to her also had a partner who did not rise to the FBI standard of quality and so he too was without a partner. His name was Timothy Yamamoto. As far as Janet was concerned, it was a pairing made in heaven. They were both fluent in Japanese and both were of mixed heritage. She was the oldest of three kids and he was the youngest of three. Although Tim was ribbed a few times about his female partner, he didn't seem to mind, especially when he and Janet won three of the top five awards in shooting and weaponry tactics.

However, it wasn't always easy. Janet remembered the time when she felt she had had enough of the locker room jokes and had almost thrown in the towel. "Maybe Carolyn Jessup was right about this being a male club," she said to the female receptionist one day. "Maybe I just don't belong here." Not waiting for any advice, she started walking down the hall but was grabbed by the arm by Tim, who ushered her into an empty room.

"Alright so you wanna give up," he said. "That's cool, but you have only three weeks left. Why are you giving these guys so much power? That's not you. At least not the you I've seen hit a target from 100 yards away, or run five miles in 30 minutes, or talk a subject out of a barricaded room. If you must play these silly games, do them in your room. You don't have to tell everyone what you're thinking. Withholding information is powerful too." He then walked away. Janet graduated three weeks later without so much as a gripe.

#

"Sorry to break up what sounds as foreign to me as the Monroe Doctrine," Howard announced casually, "but I'm headed over to the hotel because I have a more than slightly pissed off wife in Virginia who I have to speak to before she changes her will." Janet and Tim laughed heartily.

"That goes for me too," Tim added. He and Janet rose from where they had been sitting. "Well, you guys settle in" she asserted, "and I'll see you tomorrow morning at our direction summit". Howard shook her hand but Tim hugged her goodbye.

In the hotel elevator Tim's smirk made it imperative for Howard to remark "Oh yeah, this is a story you've left out!"

Tim smiled at his best friend. They got off the elevator and headed to their rooms located across the hall from each other. "Let's meet in my room in an hour to digest this info," Howard said to Tim as he put his key in the door. "Collect Waverly too."

#

30

Chapter 13

Mark Mason Watson had completed his first year of law school and felt exhausted. Howard and Carol had asked a friend, a professor at Howard University, for a favor. Without so much as a "can I see his resume?" Mark began working in the law library the following week.

If Mark required time to "figure it out", Carol and Howard wanted him do it while he was bringing in an income.

#

1987

Howard Watson was adjusting the cummerbund on his wedding tuxedo when he happened to glance in the mirror at the young man who would walk his soon-to-be wife down the aisle. Although the boy was losing the battle with his bowtie, Howard knew he would not ask for help.

Mark Mason was twelve years old and had just completed the 7th grade. He and Howard had become very good friends and Mark felt comforted by the fact that Howard and his mother were getting married. Although the previous 18 months had been traumatizing to Mark (mostly due to his father's death), therapy, and his mother's family had assisted him in making those months settle into an almost tranquil blur.

Mark and his mother Carol had moved from Chicago to Washington, D.C. to start over. A lot was riding on the move to the nation's capitol, and although his mom's family lived in D.C., Mark still felt somewhat alone. All he knew was Chicago. His friends lived in Chicago. The museums, parks, and zoos were in Chicago. Lake Michigan and the White Sox were in Chicago. Everything seemed to be in Chicago...even his father's grave.

Today, however, everything seemed to fall in place. Mark was about to walk his mother down the aisle. He was relieved that his mom had found a new husband because he hated seeing her sad. Although she told him on several occasions that she would be all right, he wondered for almost two years when that time would come.

Today was the day.

Mark was very much aware that Howard had a lot to do with his mother's happiness. Taking a sanity break from the confusion of the bowtie, he looked over at Howard, bit his lower lip and asked, "Howard would you mind if I called you Dad?"

Mark remembered Howard grabbing him and holding him for what seemed like forever.

A year later, he was ecstatic because he had become an older brother to twin boys – George and Lawrence. He was so happy that he forgot to be lonely. The birth of the twins caused the other Mark, the one he thought he left in Chicago, to come back to life big time.

Prior to graduating from elementary school Mark had set his sights on a high school that had a winning baseball team. After trying out and making the team, he settled into his studies always with the thought of law school on his mind.

In his senior year of high school, Mark received several academic, as well as athletic scholarships. He remembered vividly how that was the year something tugged at his spirit. With his mother's and Howard's blessings and especially their financial support, he decided during spring break to visit the campus of the University of Illinois, the school where his father, John Mason, and his mother had met. The U of I campus was located 2 ½ hours south of Chicago so he had to backtrack to Chicago to visit his father's grave before returning home.

He had a hard time believing eight years had passed since his father's coffin was lowered into the ground. He remembered holding his mother's hand and trying to be brave so she wouldn't break down and cry. He also remembered it was a cloudy day - unlike today.

Once Mark found his father's headstone, he took in a deep breath and then exhaled. After a few minutes, he sought energy from the sun, gave a military salute to his father's grave, and walked away.

#

Chapter 14

Janet Forrestal met the three FBI agents at the door of the conference room with a look that suggested that she had information she was dying to tell.

"Guess what?" she asked almost whispering. "Philly P.D. found a courier's briefcase!" Before the agents could digest the info, Stanton Abrams had walked into the room causing all subsequent conversation to cease.

"Agents" Abrams began, "we've just been handed a small, but maybe significant break in the courier case. Philly P.D. was given a briefcase that was found floating in the Schuylkill River in the Fairmount Park area. Forensics is i.d.'ing it now. Seems two kids were fishing in the Schuylkill when one of their lines "caught" the briefcase. Try as they might, the kids couldn't get the case open so they gave up and surrendered it to one of their parents, who in turn surrendered it to the Philly P.D."

At this point Howard and Tim were asking themselves the same question: *how did Janet know the briefcase belonged to one of the couriers?*

#

Chapter 15

Kelly Uchida hailed from a family of four kids, of which she was the youngest. Both parents were educators so education and having a family was part of her mainframe. She graduated tops in her class from a public high school in the nation's Capital and four years later magna cum laude from Georgetown University, located only three miles from her home. Feeling as if she hadn't seen the world yet, Kelly decided to venture out of her familiar cocoon for graduate school and thus chose Columbia University in New York City.

Her first day in Manhattan was exhilarating, mostly because Times Square, Broadway and Macy's were not far from Columbia's campus and she could not wait to experience them all.

Columbia University's campus was complicated. School was difficult at first because she knew *no one* and New Yorkers seemed very much in a hurry - with their views, with their schedules and with their time. Kelly learned quickly that if your speech did not improve the silence then "don't say nothin to a New Yorker."

She met Timothy Yamamoto in a molecular biology class her second week of school. She had never met a Black & Japanese person before so she was intrigued. Besides being over six feet tall, Tim was a standout from the crowd. He was so well- rounded that he reminded her of a combination of Mao, Walter Mosley and Bob Dylan. She recalled how competitive she and Tim had become, especially when she ended up with an "A" in the class and Tim received an "A" *minus*. She chuckled even though Tim did not get the joke. In spite of it all, they became good friends.

Tim was a hard nut to crack as far as women were concerned, but Kelly was able to break open his shell to find a beautiful human being. It wasn't until two years later that she decided they were in love. Despite Tim's professed adoration for her, there was no talk of marriage, or engagement, or even living together once graduate school ended. So taking a deep breath Kelly grabbed the great job offered her by Merck Pharmaceuticals in New Jersey.

#

New Jersey, in Kelly's eyes, and contrary to the New York point of view, was a beautiful state. It was only four hours long and two hours wide by car, and driving down the Garden State Parkway allowed her to experience the most breathtaking views of trees and animals that she could never recall seeing in D.C. Her favorite place to visit was Wildwood because it offered clean beaches, pizza by the slice, and just an absolute opportunity to get away from the New York/New Jersey urban tightness.

It had been more than a year since she had moved from New York City and still Tim had not mentioned marriage. He *had* mentioned that he had been accepted into the FBI Academy for which she was quite proud. *Wow, an FBI agent!*

To keep herself occupied, Kelly decided to teach a night class at Rutgers University in Newark. The several men who asked her out she deemed were either escaped convicts or just plain losers. It was almost too easy when saying "no". However, the "no's" were starting to take their toll, which subsequently made her feel like a snob, and worse. No sooner had she started saying "yes" than Tim's radar beeped and he started calling. Kelly felt that perhaps he had gotten a whiff of her going her own way. Three months later Tim proposed and asked her to move back to NYC, and in with him. One year later, they were married.

#

Carol Watson had driven Kelly to the doctor's office where she was lying in a fetal position on the table waiting to hear good news – news that her baby was fine and that the episode of pain in her lower abdomen the previous night was not serious.

She had decided to refrain from calling Tim because she knew (hoped) the pain would subside and it would turn out to be indigestion or...whatever. Unfortunately, the pain had not subsided by the time she walked hunched over into Dr. Alcott's office who immediately shipped her to George Washington University Medical Center via ambulance.

Chapter 16

Hilton Dennis was the last of eight kids born to a profane mother who hated cleaning and ironing for the rich, and an alcoholic father who barely worked during the 14 years Hilton lived under their roof. When it finally occurred to him that education was his way out of the scratch-poor community from which he hailed, Hilton applied for, and received an academic scholarship to one of the best college prep schools in the State of Pennsylvania. He left without so much as a "see ya" to his parents. He had had enough of his father's drunken, physically abusive ways, and he had had enough of his mother allowing it. Not only did his four-year scholarship take care of his academic needs, it also afforded him lodging in one of the nicest houses on the campus.

Almost immediately after arriving on the high school campus Hilton changed his name to Harry. He never wanted to have to explain to his upper-crust fellow classmates that he had been born in the laundry room of a Hilton Hotel in which his mother worked as a laundress.

#

Three things were on Julia Holland's mind: graduate school, which was going to be over in two weeks; pregnancy, as she was going to have a baby in seven months; and telling Harry Dennis she was pregnant and that he was the father of her child. Her parents were going to be furious, especially her dad, a member of the Boule', an elite Black business fraternity. Julia knew he was going to ask her why she could not at least have found a Black boyfriend. *Why couldn't I resist the arms of the devil?* He was going to throw out the usual rhetoric about being "a good girl". *Yeah, it's okay for my brothers to have sex in college but not me.* Now it had become apparent why. *Damn!*

Julia met Harry at a get-together in their first year at Pennsylvania's Wharton School of Business. Harry felt the chemistry kickin' after their initial introduction so he wasted no time in asking her out. She said "no" the first couple of times he asked, mostly because she knew her father would be furious at her for dating a white guy. *The truth?* Harry was already popular on campus, arrogant as hell, and Julia did not want him bringing what she believed was an affirmative action agenda to her life.

Somewhere along the line, she relented.

Harry Dennis had crawled out from underneath what he called "a heap of white trash". Luckily for him he was academically brilliant. He was accepted at the best prep school in Pennsylvania via a full scholarship; whizzed through Temple University, and before graduation was instantly recruited to not only Harvard but also the Wharton Business School on a full scholarship. He chose Wharton. Julia loved the way he could hold a conversation, with anyone, anytime.

Although she and Harry had emerged from two completely different upbringings, they shared the same religious beliefs and most of the time the same political beliefs, especially when it came to civil rights and getting out of Vietnam. Julia recognized early on in their relationship that Harry would never be smart enough or rich enough for her father. When she realized she was pregnant the times made her quickly dismiss the idea of abortion, but still saddled her with major difficulties – telling Harry, and telling her parents that not only that she was pregnant, but the father of her baby was white; brilliant – but white.

Harry took it all in stride. He didn't care what her parents thought of him, he adored Julia. Unfortunately, she had to make the executive decision of her young life – to refrain from revealing the father's name or his race to her parents. Harry was pissed. The two parted ways shortly thereafter especially when Harry was rudely awakened by the fact that Black people could be prejudiced too.

Julia's parents were furious with her. *Their beautiful, talented, smart, "All American" daughter was pregnant, out of wedlock…and by someone she said meant nothing to her.* It took more than a year for William Holland to come down off his perch and speak civilly to his daughter. By that time little Janet had been born and months later was able to melt his heart.

Unbeknownst to Julia, whom Harry nicknamed "Joop", he secretly kept track of her life and found out that she had given birth to a daughter…his daughter. Although he never treaded into her life, Julia somehow sensed he was around…somewhere. Years later, she had heard that Harry had graduated from law school, gone to Vietnam, and then became an FBI agent. She had also heard he never married.

When Janet turned three, Julia married Roger Forrestal, an accountant in the firm in which she worked as a CPA. Roger immediately fell in love with little Janet and instantly adopted her with Julia's blessings. Janet was now a Forrestal.

Two years later Janet became an older sister to twin brothers, Jack and Joshua. Julia now felt her life complete.

1971

Because Business School *and* Law School provided no real happiness, Harry decided to join the Army. Two months later, he was shipped to a U.S. base near the demilitarized zone in South Vietnam. A year later, and 12 days before being sent stateside, the Viet Cong captured Harry and ten of his comrades along the Cam Lo River, where they labored eight months in a POW camp. Harry and his men were finally rescued when Richard Nixon became President and brought home pretty much everyone. Harry was never the same person. Always needing something more in his life, he applied to, and was accepted into the FBI Academy.

#

At the FBI Training Academy in Quantico, Virginia, Harry took an instant liking to his roommate, Alberto Marino. They quickly set about the business of being the best all-around team. In addition to garnering several merit honors, Harry and Marino proved tops in breaking down rifles in split time. Both men were from working class poor, and both were Vietnam veterans who shared similar stories during their rare spare time. Although Marino had invited his parents to the Academy graduation, Harry invited his oldest sister and oldest brother, allowing everyone to believe *they* were his parents.

He was not surprised when he had heard the news that his father had been missing for three days when found on the side of a road in a drunken stupor. He died two days later from toxic poisoning. His mother grieved herself to death shortly thereafter without the benefit of Harry, nor any of his siblings shedding a tear.

#

PART 2

"Agents", **Abrams began.** "We had forensics go over one of the most amazing briefcases I've ever seen. We now know it belonged to that of the last courier killed. Although the Schuylkill erased any evidence of exclusive fingerprints, we know, thankfully, that fingerprints are still resistant to rough handling. We are certain this is the briefcase we've been looking for. I'd like to start off with assignments."

When Abrams finished his delivery, he motioned to Howard who slowly made his way across the room. "Because of the high security of this case," Abrams began, "I'd like for your team to accompany me to Forensics." Howard nodded affirmatively without missing a beat.

By the time Tim and Waverly arrived at the lab, evidence had already been delivered from the crime scene staff. Once the medical staff (and Tim and Waverly) visually examined the briefcase, the forensic exam took several forms: photographing the briefcase and casting an impression of several cutting marks possibly made by tool marks on the briefcase. An autopsy had already been performed by the Medical Examiner to determine the cause of Harry

Dennis' death (strangulation). It was no surprise when the M.E. handed Tim two keys she had removed from Harry's stomach. All in attendance felt confident the keys would open the briefcase. They were correct.

The briefcase had been made of a type of stainless steel unfamiliar to Tim and Waverly. It didn't suffer any damage from the Schuykyll or from the boys banging on it in their unsuccessful attempt to open it. Inside the case was one letter addressed to over seventy diamond dealers in the Philadelphia district. The letter was written in Russian. Howard would translate it later. After donning latex gloves, Abrams skimmed over the correspondence. Although he could not understand Russian, he still stopped short when he came across a name that was familiar to him - Ichiro Hasai, a well-heeled executive whose multi-billion dollar manufacturing business was headquartered in Philadelphia. Abrams placed the letter back in the briefcase and handed it to Waverly.

"I want you to bring me in a courier," he said to Tim. "I want a courier who will sing like he's in the Vienna Boy's Choir. I want a story Yamamoto, and I want one now. Is this understood?"

Tim understood. He motioned to Waverly and both agents walked through several corridors to an empty conference room.

"What do you make of the evidence Ahmad?" Tim asked once they had taken seats.

"I don't know Tim, but I'll take a stab at some scenarios. First, I have to say that this briefcase intrigues me. I've never seen a finish like this before. I don't even know if this steel comes from the U.S. Those boys couldn't have gotten this briefcase open if they torched the lock. There was no evidence at, or near the scene of Harry's or the other three courier's bodies, which leads me to believe that the killer or killers, was wearing disposable clothing, probably plastic. They most likely wore plastic on their shoes too. It would explain no defined footprints. The perpetrators knew to stand on rock instead of the dirt. Any blood that might have been shed would have been washed away by the Schuylkill." Tim nodded in agreement.

"But why would we find this briefcase downstream Tim," Waverly asked, "Unless Harry threw it in the water himself? Could that be why he was killed?"

Tim thought about it for a minute. "If you remember Ahmad, the other three couriers were also killed and no briefcase was found so I figure Harry knew they were going to kill him but he wasn't going to in any way make it easy for them."

Ahmad nodded in agreement. "I think Harry wanted us to find the briefcase; and not only did Harry want us to *find* the briefcase, he wanted us to find the two keys in his belly that would *open* the briefcase".

"Now the question is" Tim asserted, "what does Harry want us to know?

#

Chapter 18

Carol Mason's new client was big. In addition to being the Executive Vice President of a multi-billion dollar company headquartered in Philadelphia, Mr. Kukuya was willing to pay her in advance what most of her clients could only afford to pay in increments.

The case seemed simple enough: protect the company from a class action suit brought against them by twenty former employees who were fired because they were found to be illegal immigrants. The suit against them stated HMC, Inc. hired them knowing they were illegal Russian immigrants. According to Kukuya, "Each man presented the necessary, and what we thought, legal visas to our HR department which stated they could work in the United States for twelve months. This seemed fine as we only required their services for ten months."

When asked why HMC did not use their own in-house attorneys, or attorneys from Pennsylvania, the Executive Vice President stated that the CEO *personally* wanted to hire an attorney who was familiar with Japanese customs and integrity. He also wanted the case to stay out of Philadelphia and the media. Kukuya had read about Carol representing a young Japanese boy who wanted to remain in the U.S. against the wishes of his parents. He was quite fascinated that she had won the case. In addition, he thought she handled the matter with dignity for all parties involved – a Japanese tradition. He then mentioned her name to his CEO – Koriuko Hasai.

Carol thanked Kukuya profusely for the compliment but informed him that she would think it over and give him her decision the next afternoon. Kukuya requested that she accept the check anyway and if her answer would be negative, she could mail it back to the company. This way he would not have to make another trip to her office if she decided to represent the company in the lawsuit.

Carol's flag went up. Thanking him for the kind gesture, she declined the check - determined not to be bullied. Kukuya left without shaking her hand. *So much for integrity.*

#

Chapter 19

Howard read the letter.

"Если заинтересовано в свободных диамантах, встреча на пакгаузе 68024 с установленным количеством USD. Вызовите быть помещенным на списке."

He then read it aloud in English to his team.

Waverly was charged with the task of examining all fingerprints on the letters. He was also responsible for determining the origin of the steel used to create the briefcase. He would follow up on the various companies that could produce such a beauty.

#

Chapter 20

Early one evening, Nikola Gregorvsky and Ichiro Hasai met on a "no outlet" street that ended at a railroad yard. A two-story, empty, burned out warehouse was barely visible through the frames of several burned out shacks surrounding it. Maple trees lined both sides of the street. Hasai looked in several directions before he got out of the black Volvo. Gregorvsky and three other men were already in the building when Hasai and his two men, one carrying a briefcase, carefully walked into the warehouse. Hasai eyed a Cadillac parked in the building.

After Gregorvsky's men patted down Hasai and his men, Gregorvsky waited fully a minute before speaking. "I am sorry to seem the over cautious Mr. Hasai," Gregorvsky uncharacteristically stammered, "but I am in business of alert at all costs. You understand?"

"Yes, I do Mr. Gregorvsky", Hasai said without blinking. "However, should you take the liberty of "being over cautious," again with me we will have to forego this matter and move to relationships other than your own. You have insulted us twice now, and once was too many."

Gregorvsky moved past the conversation. "May I see product?" Hasai nodded slightly and motioned to one of his men to hand over a briefcase. Gregorvsky then opened it with two keys dangling around his neck. Once the briefcase was opened, 10 loose diamonds, at least five carats each, illuminated the dim evening light.

Gregorvsky looked pleased but this was only a guess. "To your liking?" Hasai asked. One of Gregorvsky's men took out of his pocket oddly shaped goggles and examined one of the diamonds. He then glanced in Gregorvsky's direction before continuing to examine the balance of the diamonds. When he had completed his mission, he looked over at Gregorvsky.

Gregorvsky spoke. "We are pleased Mr. Hasai. The rest of the inventory will go to Belgium?

"Yes, it is on its way as we speak."

"And to Norilsk?"

"Yes, Mr. Gregorvsky...as our usual plan for the past two years."

Gregorvsky signaled to his other man who produced two briefcases and handed them to Hasai.

Hasai opened one of the briefcases, took out a stack of one hundred dollar bills, flipped through it and placed the stack neatly back in its place next to the 49 other stacks. He did not open the second briefcase.

Hasai bowed. "It is our pleasure Mr. Gregorvsky. We will talk when you want." Gregorvsky bowed, and then shook Hasai's hand. Hasai then turned and walked back to the waiting Volvo. Once the car was clearly out of sight, Gregorvsky and his men got into the black Cadillac and drove away.

Two ATF agents were 200 feet away in one of the old abandoned railway cars listening to the complete conversation. Ahmad Waverly had helped with the technology.

Another set of eyes was watching the scene from another vantage point. She could also read lips. She put the binoculars down and said to the others, "They will not win *this* war."

#

Chapter 21

Kelly Yamamoto woke up in unfamiliar territory. She was in a hospital bed and trying desperately to make out the words Dr. Alcott was saying to her. Carol Watson had ridden in the ambulance with her and was now smiling at her, although the smile looked somewhat suspect. Kelly had suffered a miscarriage. *It was not your fault. You did everything right. The baby just wasn't meant to be at this time.* Kelly subsequently felt a strange but unruffled feeling surround her after being sedated. "Where is Tim?" she asked Carol. "What is he doing right now?" Dr. Alcott glanced over at Carol alerting her that Kelly was talking through an altered state. Carol whispered to Kelly that Tim was on his way. Before she could say anything else, Kelly burst into tears and then drifted into unconsciousness.

Carol gathered all the strength she could muster in order to leave the room without falling apart. Once in the hallway though she could not stop the flow of tears that fell uncontrollably. When she finally gained a sense of composure, she called Howard to relay the message to Tim.

#

Chapter 22

Howard, Tim and Ahmad were listening to the audiotape brought in from the stakeout. It was clear to all of them that they had in their grasp members of a group who were without a doubt responsible for smuggling diamonds into the area. However, they actually needed to *see* the transfer. They needed a plant - someone fluent in Japanese; someone not on Gregorvsky's or Hasai's radar; someone smart, and someone who would not flinch. Someone like Janet.

#

Howard was adamant. "Are you sure you want to do this?"

Janet did not hesitate with her answer. "Absolutely sir. Besides, whom else do we have? Sir, we need Hasai."

Howard thought a minute and looked at Tim. "What do you think?"

Tim hesitated too long.

Howard knew Tim and he knew he was thinking about the fact that Janet was a woman. An agent...but a woman. He immediately tried to adjust the situation.

"Agent Forrestal, this could prove to be a dangerous... no, it could be deadly if Gregorvsky or Hasai find out your true mission. Tim, you and Agent Forrestal are fluent in Japanese so you will have to be our buyers. Agent Forrestal, can you handle this without falling apart?"

Janet was thinking that had she been a man Howard would not have chosen those words. "Yes sir" was all she could say.

At that moment, Howard glanced at his cell phone and realized he had gotten a text message from Carol. She had put in the letters CB in uppercase letters. Howard knew that CB was their family's code blue. *What could be the emergency? Please tell me nothing has happened to the boys or my parents.*

#

Stanton Abrams was not happy with the news. He did not believe Forrestal was ready for Lead Agent status. She was ready for high caliber work, but not as lead - not yet. Nevertheless, when Howard completely described the mission Abrams succumbed to the fact that if Forrestal would be going for the kill, at least a seasoned veteran like Yamamoto would have her back. He gave in.

"Okay, listen up Agents" Jergensen began. "I want to make this clear to all of you. Forrestal has to be covered every inch of the way. She will be buying and Yamamoto will be her backup. We will work out details later this afternoon. Holloway, I will need passports for Forrestal and Yamamoto – new names from California. We also need an African passport for Waverly." Howard glanced over at Waverly who was an inch away from smiling. "Ahmad, I'm going to need some type of monitoring device, something embedded in a stone, not a real diamond, but some type of valuable looking stone that Forrestal can wear as a ring. It has to be flawless looking but not necessarily real. We need to know her whereabouts at all times. Got it?"

"Got it" Waverly answered.

Jergensen articulated his concerns. "We want video, so Carlson and Woods, stay on Hasai. We'll track Gregorvsky. I don't want to know that Hasai sneezed without you being close enough to say bless you. Get me?"

Both agents nodded affirmatively.

"Howard, I want to meet with you in the conference room. We'll discuss further how to make sure Waverly connects with the Africans." Howard nodded. "Everyone dismissed."

#

Chapter 23

Ichiro Hasai had no way of knowing Harry Dennis had died when Patrice Asgedom requested a meeting with him. Usually Harry would be the person to collect facts and data on an individual and supply this communication to him. If the person was deemed "clean", Ichiro would move on it. If not, no form of communication would ever take place. Ichiro hadn't heard from Harry in over a week. *At this time*, he wasn't overly concerned because Harry could sometimes stay underground for weeks. Ichiro had to move on and besides, Harry was becoming a problem with his drinking. The only reason he kept him employed was their longtime association.

Ichiro hated to admit it, but Harry was the only person he knew who could find the intermediaries who could get diamonds cleaned up for sale, then get them "certified", and lastly get them into the U. S. under the radar. At issue now was yet *another* new warlord named Patrice Asgedom who had wrestled the title from the previous warlord. Now Ichiro had to deal with *him* in order to keep his diamond mine, and especially his profits, out of African hands.

Ichiro had received conflicting information on Asgedom, and he really needed Harry's expertise in getting the correct and accurate information for him. Ichiro's inner sanctum advised him to hold off with Asgedom until he met with Harry, but Ichiro was faced with yet another "partner" and Harry was nowhere to be found.

Ichiro felt he had no choice but to resort to secondary detecting sources. Harry's gift was always being able to get the "warlord in charge" to permit Ichiro to continue his ownership of Seigo-sei Mining Company. Ichiro had paid millions of dollars to the Africans to protect all areas of his operation, but especially his equipment and transportation. Without asking, the Congolese warlords were always kind enough to take their share *first*.

Asgedom, according to two of Ichiro's sources, was a gem specialist, born in Ethiopia, but worked behind the scenes in Joseph Mobutu's Congolese government where corruption was rampant. When the Soviet Union collapsed and the U.S. no longer needed Mobutu, Asgedom quickly escaped to Ethiopia. Several years later, he was found living in Miami, Florida.

Against his better judgment, Ichiro scheduled a meeting with Asgedom in Miami...but not before putting the word out to find Harry Dennis.

\#

Chapter 24

When Tim received word of Kelly's miscarriage a wave of anxiety surrounded him. He didn't know what to do or say to her to make her feel better. Although he was relieved... that she was physically ok, he also experienced guilt and thought perhaps he should fly home to be with her for a couple of days. Howard felt the same way.

#

Chapter 25

Nikola Gregorvsky was making plans to meet Ichiro Hasai in Miami. He had just returned from his parent's residence near Norilsk, Russia, home to the biggest source of nickel in the world. Gregorvsky traded nickel for diamonds with Hasai because nickel was the key strengthening ingredient in stainless steel. Gregorvsky's people in Russia were in charge of melting the nickel and then converting it into solid form. Hasai used the nickel, now converted into stainless steel, in his appliance manufacturing plants. Gregorvsky used the diamonds to influence cyber crime gangs, global drug trafficking and small governments opposed to Russian interests. The relationship was a match made in Russia...the same as if it was made in hell.

As much as Gregorvsky enjoyed the accolades associated with being the brains behind a lot of information, he frankly had never heard of Patrice Asgedom. He was intrigued, but not concerned. His felt relatively confident his comrades in Brooklyn would find out everything about Asgedom. In addition, they would scout out Miami where he and Ichiro would meet with the Congolese warlord.

#

Howard placed calls to the Brooklyn and Miami FBI offices while Bruce Jergensen met with CIA to make sure their "Patrice Asgedom" was legitimately knowledgeable and no room for slip-ups could occur. All offices understood the magnitude of a missed step. Miami office immediately set up an apartment and jewelry front for Asgedom, while Brooklyn office planted info about Asgedom on a "secret" international website; a website that the unenlightened would be shocked to learn operated exclusively out of a closet in a FBI office in Quantico, Virginia.

Ahmad met with the M-E's office to assist with researching the origin of the steel briefcase. They realized that if Harry Dennis had not posthumously forked over the keys for them they probably would not have gotten the briefcase open without severely damaging not only the case, but also, more importantly – its contents.

#

Ahmad, Howard and Janet spent the next three days with CIA agents, including "Patrice Asgedom." They also met with two master gemologists who specialized in diamonds. Karl Kregl, one of the master diamond cutters, informed the agents "Agent Asgedom's knowledge has to be accepted as well informed - answering questions in a general way. He doesn't have to be a gemologist to be a salesperson, nor an oligarch to run various factions in the Congo, he just has to *appear* as if he is a rogue tyrant and that would prove satisfactory."

There are four "C's" to diamonds," he continued. They are cut, clarity, color and carat weight. Sometimes we add a fifth "C" for certificate."

"Which is the most important "C"? Howard asked.

"Cut, so it is important to understand how this quality affects the properties and values of a diamond. A good cut gives a diamond its brilliance. Agent Asgedom I would like you to take a look at the three rings in front of you and tell me which one is the diamond."

Asgedom looked at the three rings on the black velvet fingers. He picked up each one, looked at the settings, peered through the stones, felt their weight and finally came up with his guess. He then pointed to one of the rings.

"Agent Waverly, would you do the same thing please?"

Ahmad picked a different ring.

"Agent Forrestal, would you also do me the honor of choosing the real one please?"

Janet picked the same ring as Asgedom.

Kregl smiled. "Agent Waverly you picked a stone called cubic zirconium. If it is mounted in a good quality setting you will need to consult an experienced jeweler to assess if the stone is real."

He looked over at Janet and winked while shaking his head. "Agent Forrestal, you and Agent Asgedom picked a stone called moissanite. It was made in a laboratory. But, and this is an important but, it was a terrific guess on both your part as moissanite gems are nearly flawless. Moissanite is even more difficult than zirconium to tell from a real diamond yet it costs only one-tenth the price of a diamond. As you can see, it is virtually indistinguishable from the real diamond and it takes a real expert with special equipment to tell the difference. This is also the stone that *you* Agent Forrestal will be wearing. In addition, Agent Asgedom you will be selling these out of your black market shop in Florida."

"If you can make absolutely beautiful stones like this out of a lab, why do diamonds cost so much?" Janet asked.

Dexl Bruhn, the other gemologist answered. "There are

so many lies associated with diamonds that it would take all day to debunk most of them. The popular ones start with the proclamation that diamonds are rare. They are not. Diamonds are so plentiful in that, there are enough for each person in the U.S. to have quite a few."

"Another lie is that people think diamonds are a great investment – which they are not. Don't take my word for it. Try to sell your diamond ring to a pawnshop or even on eBay. Diamonds are not a girl's best friend, but they certainly are a jeweler's best friend!"

"You mentioned that there is also a fifth "C"? Howard asked.

"Yes," Kregl acknowledged. "The fifth "C" is for certificate. The Gemological Institute of America or American Gem Society certifies most diamonds. A certificate tells you the diamond's exact measurements and weight as well as the details of its cut and quality. The certificate also serves as proof of the diamond's identity and value. At this time, sight-holders, or the 79 authorized rough diamond-dealing families worldwide, do not keep track of the origin of every diamond that passes through their facilities. So really, nobody can tell you with any accuracy where a diamond was sourced from, and anyone that tells you he can is probably lying.

#

Chapter 26

"Agents", Howard began. "We have a situation."

All the agents had gathered the next morning for the meeting and sat down immediately.

"We were informed from DMV and Social Security that somebody is checking on Asgedom's identity. This means the "who's" are working on finding out if our plant is a plant. We need to get to our man in the Congo. We also need to talk with our people in Eritrea."

Bruce Jergensen broke in. "Howard, Abrams told me last night that our people shifted positions to Ethiopia."

"Why?"

"Because Eritrea will be at war with Ethiopia soon and the U.S. will likely have to act as a go-between. For now Central Ops thought it best to be on the side of Ethiopia."

How does Stanton know these two countries will be at war soon? Howard tried his best not to think naively.

"Howard", Jergensen continued, "CIA will be meeting with us this afternoon. Be ready with questions."

#

Five hours later, everyone on Howard's task team, except Tim, was present. The CIA agents marched through the glass doors on time, pretty much to everyone's delight. Jergensen received a nod from one of the CIA Ops and quickly had one of his men close the drapes in order to show the short video. The video revealed very young children working in a diamond mine in Africa. The Ops imparted the following while the video played:

"Even though the country does not have an official diamond mining industry, the Congo somehow is able to export large quantities of diamonds in addition to falsifying certificates of origin. Children, anywhere in age from six to twelve are the most important employees of the various mining companies. Why you ask? In addition, why so young? Adults and teenagers understand the value of the diamonds and try on a consistent basis to steal one or two for themselves. Young children understand they are working to help support their families and will not accept as true that the rocks they are hauling in for the various factions carry more value than their paychecks."

The video continued while Howard and other agents who were fathers became uncomfortable watching the video.

Finally, it was over. The Ops continued. "We have been handed information that a businessman here in Philadelphia named Ichiro Hasai is an owner of a rough diamond trading firm in the Congo. More importantly, Hasai shares the profits of his bounty with a certain Russian thug named Nikola Gregorvsky. Ever hear of either of them?" Many in the room nodded.

"Good", the Ops continued, "Because they are who we need to rein in."

Janet looked at Howard for permission to ask a question. "You do realize of course that Hasai is worth at least four billion dollars and it seems almost absurd to believe he *personally* has his hand in the destruction of any country."

This was a question all the agents wanted to ask.

"Good point. Agent Forrestal, I believe?" Janet nodded.

"There's an old saying Agent Forrestal and it goes like this. "More money makes more of who you really are." Hasai is greedy. We have been watching him and Gregorvsky ever since another thug from Russia named Yuri Rostovsky was deported back to Siberia. Typical Russian that he is, Gregorvsky didn't learn from Rostovsky's defeat. Gregorvsky is definitely working under the radar with Congolese warlords. He is very talented. Of the two men though - Rostovsky and Gregorvsky, I would have picked Rostovsky to be running the outfit. Obviously, I am wrong. *The problem with Gregorvsky* is that he actually believes he will not get caught because of the depth of Hasai's pockets. *The problem with Ichiro Hasai* is that his old man knows nothing about his son's dealings in Africa. But he will, and Japanese honor will soon be put to the test."

#

Chapter 27

Despite the miscarriage, Kelly was physically able to go home from the hospital late that afternoon. Dr. Alcott told her and Tim that she had a "weak cervix and it had widened releasing the fetus without warning signs of labor." Before taking her home, the doctor told them "Kelly could still have a chance at a full labor...prevention of a future miscarriage would call for corrective surgery on the uterus and a stitch in the cervix to keep it from widening."

The emotional toll on Kelly was something Tim's mother told him would lessen if Tim were around. After four days of being around, Tim wanted to be in Philadelphia with the rest of the law enforcement team. He wanted to feel something besides captivity.

He couldn't believe Kelly told both sets of parents that she was pregnant without consulting him first. He couldn't believe that she wanted a baby so badly that she would go against their plan of agreeing first.

He also could not believe how egotistical he sounded. This wasn't about *him*. This was about Kelly - who had never lied about wanting a baby; who had never lied about her love for him, and who had never lied about how excited she was when she found out she was pregnant.

For the next several days, Kelly sensed remoteness from Tim that she had never felt before. She couldn't explain it, but the fact remained that they had barely spoken two paragraphs worth of words. She believed Tim wanted to be gone. Not just from Virginia, but from her.

Tim did not want a baby. *At least not now.* Kelly had asked how long she had to wait. Although he couldn't answer the question right away, he did think seriously about his answer. *I just don't want another reason to be home. This is going to hurt her deeply.*

#

Chapter 28

Carol Watson was deeply concerned about the very well-to-do client she turned down. Mr. Kikuyu, as promised, left her alone after she said no to his proposition to represent HMC, Inc.

She was relieved after talking with Howard who informed her that he thought it a good chess move for *Hasai's* firm to approach her. He was unbelievably glad she had asked his advice first about signing on to this case. Had she accepted the retainer, even later to give it back, Hasai's lawyers could have yelled conflict of interest and Howard would have been pulled off the case. Howard later mentioned this set-up to Bruce Jergensen who agreed that Hasai's people were probably rogue Philly cops who found out Howard was married to an attorney.

The operation continued to move ahead, but it was agreed to by the higher ups that Philadelphia P.D. would be excluded from further privileged communication.

\#

Chapter 29

The three men ran out of the alley. One was armed with a briefcase as they headed toward a waiting black Jeep. "Done" was all that was said to the female driver as they sped away. They took off their plastic clothing and balled them up. When the female driver had driven at least five miles from the alley, each man threw his clothing into a different dumpster.

In the alley, a man's body was lying on the ground with chain link around his neck. Inside the breast pocket of his suit jacket was a note which read," If you find my body, the briefcase is missing."

#

Chapter 30

Stanton Abrams brought the assemblage to attention by introducing CIA Ops Supervisor Rick Keaton. "Agents", he began. "By now you have gone through your information packets and are more than familiar with the term "blood diamonds". I am only here to apprise you of several facts on just why we are dealing with the Congo."

"First, a little history."

"The discovery of oil on the Congolese coast in the early part of the 20th century by the French was a blessing – to France that is. For most of the local population, it was a curse. France made all the money, and the Congolese made it all possible. The Congo is now busy trying to make sure no other outsider garners more from their backs than they do.

The Congo's history with natural resources doesn't just rest in oil. Their history with diamonds goes back a long way too. The main reason for their civil wars is due to the diamond trade. The African continent supplies more than 45% of the world's diamonds and the Congo is a prime region. The people of the Congo have been taken for a ride again, but this time they are generating wealth for men they believe have their best interest at heart. The only thing these so-called "next rulers" have at heart is money, because money brings power. These insurgents are arming themselves with the latest weapons and ammunition in order to be the next oppressor. Unfortunately, the true power in the Congo is economic power and it lies in the hands of diamond mine owners, who most certainly are not the warlords."

Keaton paused.

"Understand I'm not about to tell my wife to take off her diamond because of the lie fed to her and 90% of the women around the world by the diamond industry. I'm also not about to remind *The Director* that African citizens are being tortured and separated from their families to mine this lie. I am however going to tell you that we have to find the couriers coming into the states. No matter what the jeweler says, he cannot be sure of the authenticity of his diamonds and he also can't be certain that his diamonds did not buy ammunition for a splinter group bent on revolution."

"The Congo is one of the top suppliers of diamonds to the United States, so we are setting our sights on four particular diamond mine owners living in Texas, Nevada, Utah, and Pennsylvania, specifically here in Philadelphia. Which is why we are starting with Mr. Ichiro Hasai."

Once Keaton finished talking, he asked for questions.

"Just to be clear", one of the DEA agents, asked, "are we saving the Congo from predator revolutionists, or are we saving the diamond industry from total collapse of credibility?"

Keaton thought about the question. "Good question. Although I am not an economic hit man, I am going to take a personal step here by saying the U.S. has always been viewed as paternal. I believe we like this view of ourselves – always ready to step in and *save* some country from itself.

However lately we seem to be defending the wrong sibling. The Congo needs our help, sure, but we can no longer afford to defend countries that are not only fighting internally, but also then turn around and start fighting us. No way, no more...I hope. This is strictly an opinion.

A question came from the corner of the room. "Do we have a specific strategy for putting a leash on the diamond industry?"

"No, because we don't regulate the way a company does business unless it is doing something illegal. The jewelers receive certificates of authenticity from their suppliers. They have to believe the certs to be legitimate. We are after the suppliers as they function purely as liaison to the diamond mine owners."

"Somewhere between the diamond mine owner and the retailer the consumer gets shafted. If people, especially in this country, stop buying personal diamonds, I suppose the retailers would be much more discriminating when it comes to purchasing them. At this time, it ain't happening! This country was built on the free enterprise system. We will not rock the boat. Any more questions? No? Agents, thank you for your time."

Bruce Jergensen thought Keaton had answered the questions far better than he would have. Stanton Abrams escorted Keaton to another meeting as Howard and Bruce Jergensen's teams stayed behind.

Once the Philly P.D. and DEA partners left the room, Jergensen announced, "Another courier's body was found. We have to find out who is the enemy of our enemy."

#

Chapter 31

Miami FBI took over a fledgling jewelry business on an ordinary street in a run of the mill strip mall. The shop came complete with several days' worth of trash and register receipts in the dumpster in the parking lot behind the stores. Patrice Asgedom and two other CIA operatives, now well versed on gems, were ready.

#

Janet studied her new passport and her new name, Cassandra Davenport, and was intrigued by the sound of it. She was relieved that Tim was back on the case and could now finish the assignment with her. His name had been changed to William Hiyashi. Their names would take time to uncover as fake.

#

Howard wanted to brief the team on their assignments and bring them up to date on the most recent courier killing. He called for a late meeting in his suite.

"Agents", he began. "Another courier's body was found yesterday. This time the killers were a bit sloppy. The one footprint discovered near the body did not belong to the victim."

"How do you know it was a courier Howard?" Ahmad asked.

"Because he had the same note on him the others had and no briefcase was found. Someone, or *someone's*, not sure which yet, has made killing couriers an almost frightening sport. We have to find out who is getting rid of these men and why. Ahmad, have you found anything concrete regarding the manufacturer of the steel briefcases?"

"No Howard...not yet. However, I did find out that the steel is foreign made. I'd say within a day or two we'll probably know where this steel came from."

"Tim, I want you and Forrestal to get to Miami, keeping an eye on Asgedom's shop so you will know when to stop in and buy. We have a two-bedroom apartment set up for you two. Ahmad and Holloway, I want you two to go today. Your apartment will be located directly across the hall from Yamamoto and Forrestal's. Both apartments have clear, but different views of Asgedom's store. Your cell phones will be at the apartments. Miami office will give you instructions. Call when you have settled in. That's it unless there are any questions."

"What do you need from us once we get to Miami?" Ahmad asked.

"I need a number of things Ahmad. First, some type of listening or video device not only for Forrestal and Yamamoto, but also for Bruce and me. Second, we will need rings for the jewelry store. They cannot be real Ahmad as I'm sure Chief would split his neck veins explaining real jewelry that could easily vanish. Miami will set you up in their lab. Those guys are good."

"Third, I want Tim and Forrestal's rental car to have all the bells and whistles you can place on it to make sure *no one* gets close enough to them without their or our knowledge."

"Holloway, you'll be working with Ahmad in the Miami office. They know you and you know the area. Make sure that around the clock tabs on Forrestal and Yamamoto are in place. I want Gregorvsky. Jergensen and I will be near."

"That's it. Get a good night's rest and your rides will pick you up at 0600 hours for flights to Miami International."

#

Chapter 32

When Howard and Bruce Jergensen's plane landed in Miami, Ahmad and Gil Holloway had already spent more than 21 hours in the Miami lab working with other scientists on simulated gems. They seemed ready to impart good news. Ahmad introduced Howard to the head chemist, Eliot Denny, a longhaired Ph.D. His thick Bahamian accent was almost melodic.

Denny then introduced Howard and Jergensen to the rest of his team who seemed thrilled to be working on simulated gems, especially diamonds. Realizing the gems had to be top quality, the chemists had to create the type of stone that even a first class gemologist would have a difficult time challenging its authenticity. Howard wanted to know why the team chose moissanite.

"A number of reasons Agent Watson" Dr. Denny began. "First, just like most diamonds, moissanite is almost colorless. It's the second hardest gem on earth right behind a diamond but interestingly its brilliance is greater than a diamond's. Even though rhinestones and cubic zirconium try to imitate the beauty of diamonds, mostly at a lower cost, they lack the luster and brilliance of the real thing. Moissanite is so brilliant that even a skilled jeweler cannot easily distinguish it from a diamond."

"Well if this stone is so perfect," Howard asked, "why don't we see more of them in the stores?"

"Moissanite is made of silicon carbide Agent Watson, and is available only as a lab creation because its natural state isn't found on earth."

"What do you mean *not found on earth*?" Jergensen asked with a somewhat quizzical look on his face.

Ahmad answered. "Dr. Denny means that moissanite fragments were originally found in an ancient meteorite, somewhere I believe, in Arizona in the late 19th century."

"Yes" Dr. Denny continued, "This stone can be easily produced in the laboratory from everyday ingredients and moissanite costs one-tenth of whatever a diamond costs. However, most of its cost isn't in the stone but actually in the jewelry setting. Moissanite is manufactured through a patented thermal growing process, the specifics of which are proprietary. The *process* is very difficult and expensive, thus preventing mass production. Only one company in the U.S. has this patented process and they are not budging."

"Still there is great news," Ahmad said to Howard.

Howard then half glanced at Waverly. "Oh yeah? Tell me more because this stone sounds too terrific to be real."

"It's pretty terrific Howard". Ahmad answered. "But as Dr. Denny explained to Gil and me, moissanite does have one disadvantage as a gem…"

Dr. Denny broke in…"it's birefringent."

Everyone, including Ahmad, looked at Dr. Denny.

"I'm sorry, birefringent means you split one ray of light into two. Under certain conditions, moissanite may give the viewer a sense of double vision. Also, naturally occurring moissanite forms very small crystals so our chemists can only synthesize silicon carbide in small stones."

Holloway broke in. "A company in the U.S. has invented a piece of equipment that can tell the difference between moissanite and diamond. *Right now* the device is expensive but the cost will no doubt come down within a few years."

Ahmad interrupted. "Howard, what we have going for us at this time is that most consumers haven't even heard of moissanite yet, so our hope is that our Mr. Gregorvsky is one of them and brings only his jeweler's goggles."

After the mini seminar, the group took a tour of the lab and later watched, in amazement, the manufacture of Janet Forrestal's "wedding rings".

#

Janet and Tim's plane landed in Miami later that day. They headed to their apartment and settled in. In Janet's, as well as Tim's room, a cell phone was waiting for them on their dresser. A number was taped to the back of both phones. Both agents called the number and were given an identification number. They were also given another phone number to call. After calling the second number, Howard answered Tim's call and Stanton Abrams answered Janet's call.

"Glad you made it in okay Tim," Howard said. Right now, we are at the Miami lab just finishing Agent Forrestal's wedding rings. Hope she likes them."

#

Chapter 33

Nikola Gregorvsky could not remember the last time he was afraid of anything. He recognized early in his life that just being able to escape the severity and bleakness of Russia was scary enough. However, working in collaboration with "the Jap" made him uncomfortable...but not scared. Hasai was so smug that sometimes it infuriated Gregorvsky. *Everything seems to come so easy for him.* Although he truly enjoyed making tons of money with Hasai, Gregorvsky did not trust him. Then again, Gregorvsky didn't trust anyone. Communism had a way of building a shell around him and everyone else he knew who had escaped from the Russian definition of Satan: Stalin.

He was returning to the U.S. after visiting his father and sister in Norilsk, Russia. His mother, bless her heart, had died many years earlier and although Gregorvsky still had a sister left in Russia to take care of their father, Gregorvsky knew his father needed to touch his face at least twice a year. His father was 87 but could still out muscle the 60 year-old Gregorvsky in a no-holds barred arm wrestling match.

Russia was hard on men, but seemed harder on women.

Maybe because so many widows and fatherless children were left lifeless due to Russia's mishandling of many wars. Gregorvsky's father had been a classical violinist *forced* to retire to become a laborer. His mother had been a teacher of languages. Gregorvsky and his two older siblings loved listening to her converse in four languages with little effort. Soon they too learned foreign languages with ease. The students loved Gregorvsky's mother; she brought sunshine into their dreary lives...yet she could not save her own.

Gregorvsky's brother spoke out one too many times against Stalin, and was eventually banished to a Gulag work camp. The family never saw him again. Gregorvsky's sister, who never married, felt the same way about Stalin the devil but eventually became too afraid to say anything. She suffered silently and finally became mute to everyone except her brother and parents.

After the banishment of her eldest son, Gregorvsky's mother slowly let the sunshine slip from her face. She later developed a nasty cough teaching near the nickel plant in Norilsk, one of the most polluted places on earth. Here the snow was always black and the air smelled like sulfur. Just as the family was financially able to pay for a doctor, Gregorvsky's mother's cough had developed into black lung. She died at age 47; Gregorvsky was 20.

#

Chapter 34

The driver of the black Jeep drove to an area just outside Philadelphia's city limits. After making sure no one had followed her, she turned onto a gravel road and stopped the vehicle. She slid from the driver's seat and jumped out of the SUV. Her three male companions also scrambled out of the Jeep. She carried the stainless steel briefcase down four steps to the basement of an abandoned boarded up house with the three men in tow. The only other building on the block was located across the street. It too was boarded up.

Using a key, she opened the basement door and went straight to a door hidden behind piled up crates and boxes. She moved them aside with ease. Housed inside the closet-like room were three other steel briefcases lying on the floor. She threw the newest briefcase on top of the others. She closed the door putting the crates and boxes back in front of the closet.

"Ain't you gonna look inside them?" one of the men asked. "No" she answered. "I know what's inside them: hopelessness, despair, depression...lies. None of these are good for my people." She then gave each man two hundred dollars. They all returned to the Jeep and drove off.

Two ATF agents were perched atop a radio tower dressed in utility uniforms and both were peering through binoculars made especially for this occasion. "Who do you suppose they are?" one agent asked the other. "I believe someone said they are the enemy of our enemy," he answered. "We need to call Agent Jergensen."

#

"Did you get a good look at them?" Bruce asked. He was talking to the agents who had followed the Jeep. Sitting on the balcony outside his hotel room in the sweltering Miami heat made him quickly realize he had made a mistake taking the call outside.

"We're not really sure of a lot of things sir," one agent offered. "The driver was a Black woman, 20-25 years old. We estimate the three men with her to be the same age. Sir, we did manage to get a license plate."

While fanning himself like a woman experiencing a hot flash, this bit of news made Jergensen feel optimistic. "Good work. What do you suppose they were doing in the building?"

Agent Woods answered. "We don't know sir, but the woman went into the house with a shiny looking briefcase and emerged not more than 10 minutes later without it."

"Tell me what you find inside that house Agent Woods. I need to know."

"Yes sir. We will be heading to the house as soon as we see the Jeep leave."

Woods put away his phone while Carlson continued to peer through his binoculars. "Let's go," he said, placing his binoculars back in its case on his shoulder. They climbed down from the radio tower, got in a dark gray SUV and drove to the abandoned building. Using his binoculars again, Carlson glanced in all directions before getting out of the vehicle.

Secure in the thought that they were not being followed, nor was anyone left in the house, they parked the SUV in the back of the building. A loose board on one of the first floor windows made it easy for the agents to pry it off quickly and let themselves into the house. Both agents kept their hand on their gun, now locked and loaded.

Although it was daylight, it was dark inside the house so Woods pulled out a flashlight to light the way. They descended the stairs to the basement but saw only empty crates and boxes in a corner. They headed back up to the main floor, looked through several empty rooms, and then headed upstairs. They searched feverishly through the three bedrooms and closets for the briefcase knowing that the woman did not have it when she returned to the vehicle. *She had to have left it in the house* Woods said aloud.

They headed back downstairs when Woods noticed a cell phone vibrating on the kitchen counter.

He looked over at Carlson but before they had a chance to talk, a vehicle pulled up in front of the building - it was the black Jeep. Both agents darted into the closet in the hallway...just in time.

"How could you have left that phone?" a male voice asked. "You know she won't pay us no more if we make another mistake."

"I don't know man," another male voice answered. "It must have been when I went to take a leak. Anyway, there it is." The owner of the phone retrieved his property and the men quickly left the building. Woods and Carlson exhaled. When they heard the vehicle pull off, Woods called Bruce with details.

"We did not find the briefcase Agent Jergensen" Woods

relayed. "We believe we looked everywhere. The basement is empty except for what looks like empty boxes and crates. We checked all the bedrooms, kitchen cabinets and appliances, closets and bathrooms. All are empty."

Carlson broke in. "Agent Jergensen, our search was interrupted when two of the men returned to retrieve a cell phone. We will attempt to lift prints off the bathroom doorknob."

"Agents, do me a favor?" Bruce asked.

"Sure, anything sir," Woods answered.

"Let me know what's in the crates and boxes in the basement."

After Bruce finished talking with the ATF agents, he stepped back into his room to get out of the heat.

#

"Howard, I believe we have the information you wanted about the briefcase." It was Ahmad on the other end of the receiver. Howard appreciated his calm demeanor. "I'll bring the information by this evening."

"Good work Ahmad. I can read it over dinner. We can eat in my room…say 7p.m. I'll also call in Jergensen, Tim, Forrestal and Holloway."

#

Chapter 35

"Если заинтересовано в свободных диамантах, встрече на пакгаузе 68024 с установленным количеством USD. Вызовите быть помещенным на списке"

Since the letter was written in Russian Howard read to himself first. Afterwards he put it down and looked as if he was contemplating reading further. He then spewed out the following: "According to Ahmad, the steel was manufactured in Russia, but the briefcase was assembled in the United States. Guess where?"

All agents looked intrigued.

"Hasai Manufacturing Company."

He then translated the letter for the others. "If interested in loose diamonds, meet at warehouse 68024 with the established amount of USD. Call to be placed on the list."

"Where do you suppose warehouse 68024 is Howard?" Tim asked.

"I have no idea Tim," he answered. "Let's check to see if it's a zip code, especially a zip code or address of one of

Hasai's plants. Holloway, you and Forrestal ever hear of this warehouse?"

Both shook their heads no. "Could it be a combination of numbers Howard?" Holloway asked.

"Don't know Gil," he answered. "I now know one thing for sure, no matter what jewelers tell us, some of them know exactly where their diamonds are coming from. This is not good news. We might have to shake up a few to get a name, or at least a place and time. Since there was no number in the instructions, we are guessing these jewelers already have the number. I would say start with those jewelers of Russian persuasion. Bruce, can you help with this without getting Philly P.D.'s flag up?"

Jergensen nodded while dialing Stanton Abram's phone number.

Before anyone could offer any further suggestions, Jergensen's cell phone vibrated - it was Agent Woods. When Bruce finished talking to him, he announced to the group, "Woods and Carlson found the other briefcases. All we need now is to put the several pieces of this puzzle in their correct places. Perhaps then we'll have a picture of what we're dealing with. Also, that zip code is located in Oaxaca, Mexico. "Let's get Keaton on this to see if Hasai is doing any business in beautiful, serene, quiet Oaxaca that we need to know about. "

"Thanks for the quick info Bruce" Howard exclaimed. "By the way, we might have found "the enemy of our enemy". Want to go over again what we have?"

#

Chapter 36

"Tim, I haven't been able to ask you about Kelly. How is she, and how are you?" Both Janet and Tim were sipping drinks on their veranda. Both alcoholic beverages produced the same stimulating effects.

"Janet, you know me, this isn't going to be easy to talk about. I mean, Kelly is okay, physically speaking."

"Sorry Tim, I didn't mean to irritate you. We don't have to talk about this. I just thought you might want to get this off your head so that your focus is not clouded."

"My focus is not clouded Janet. Actually, I feel so clear right now that it bothers me. I've been such an ass about not wanting kids that I haven't been able to see beyond anyone's needs but my own. I've been justifying my feelings for 10 years now and it has certainly worked for me. Kelly has known this all our married life."

Janet looked over at her friend and colleague. "Tim, I need your complete attention on this case or else I have to mention to Agent Watson to ship you back to Quantico. No way can I let you work this case with this kind of obstruction on your head. You hear me?"

Tim nodded, nursing his drink. "Janet I need you to go with me on this. Can you?" She nodded reluctantly.

"I love being an agent" he began. "Marriage is something my mother and father believe in and have believed in from the day they met." He took another drink. "I adore Kelly. I don't believe there is another woman…"

Janet looked out over the water.

"…I can truly say is more of a soul mate than Kelly. But, I know she will leave me if I tell her…" He stopped talking.

"Tell her what Tim?" Janet asked.

"Tell her how much I love my job. This is what I live for. I love being on the go, running to wherever a case takes me - Chicago, D.C., Mexico, Philly…wherever. I love this. I know it sounds crass, maybe unbelievably selfish but I love being on the go Janet. I'd be an idiot if I didn't believe that looking forward and not seeing Kelly by my side would produce a lonely man. Right now Janet, I'm not that man."

Janet took another drink. *I wish I could hold you right now Tim because I feel the same way.*

Of course, she wasn't going to tell him this. *Not now anyway.*

#

At 3:00 a.m. Janet was having a hard time sleeping. She kept thinking about the courier on the slab in Philly. *What was it about him that seemed familiar to me?* She knew she had never met the person; his name wasn't familiar either. *Why do I feel as if I know him?* She glanced over at the clock and realized to her dismay that it was now only 3:05 a.m. She decided to think about her mother who would be hosting a garden party later that afternoon. The thought of such a boring affair finally allowed her to doze off.

#

The sound of Tim's voice in the next room woke her up at 6:00 a.m. He seemed to be arguing with someone on the phone. Janet reasoned it was his wife. When the conversation became somewhat heated, she placed a pillow over her head and tried to go back to sleep. What seemed like only five minutes later was really an hour later. Her alarm clock on her cell phone would not let up so she forced herself to get out of the bed… grudgingly.

She dragged into the kitchen with the thought of making coffee but Tim had already beaten her to it. She was determined not to mention the fact that Tim's loud conversation kept her from getting a truly satisfying sleep.

Tim would not let her off easily. "Janet, I know you heard me yelling on the phone last night…"

"This morning" she corrected him.

"This morning" he winced. I'm sorry...truly sorry. It won't happen again."

Janet glanced over at Tim who looked as if he hadn't slept at all. She saw something that frightened her. In the FBI Academy, it was drilled into the trainees that emotions were something that an agent could not afford to let creep into his or her life...at least not on the job. *Misplaced emotions were not friends to an agent and ruined the ability to think clearly and to focus.* Tim was emotional, but Janet felt he was not afraid of the danger of this case. He was afraid of something else. A knock on the door caused her to refrain from this line of questioning with Tim. It was Howard, followed by Ahmad and Gil.

"Good" he said. "You're both up. We need to talk."

Howard poured himself a cup of coffee while setting a box of donuts on the table. He also produced the most gorgeous ring Janet had ever seen. Her mouth must have fallen open because Howard smiled. She caught how goofy she must have looked and toned down the smile a notch. "Sorry" she said with a chuckle.

"Not a problem Janet" he said with a slight laugh. "Agents" he began. "This is the ring Janet will be wearing when she and Tim visit Asgedom's shop. Janet, Ahmad has placed inside the setting a chip that will allow us to keep constant surveillance on you."

Although Howard motioned to Ahmad, he was looking at Tim quizzically.

"Agent Forrestal, you *cannot* let this ring get wet" Ahmad began. "Which means you'll have to remove it before you take a shower or bath or get in the pool. If it gets wet, it will take 1-2 hours to dry out to become operable again. The chip is located in the setting so even if you were to lose the gem, God forbid, we can still monitor your whereabouts."

"Is this stone a moissanite?" Janet asked. "Yes" Ahmad answered. "Also, the same kind of monitoring device is located on the back bumper of your and Tim's rental car. If someone decides to follow you, you will know. The camera is located on the middle of the bumper, and it will take pictures of the car behind you. Whoever is tailing you will never know you know it. Not only will the camera get the license plate of the car, but a picture of the driver and front passenger as well."

Tim spoke up. "Ahmad, how many exposures can the camera take? I mean if 50 cars are behind us today, and we don't want to tip off anyone how will we know which car is the actual one following us?"

"Tim, we will look at the exposures daily. If we see the same car or cars more than we should we can probably narrow it down to one or several cars tailing you. By the way, we have to activate both of your voices, as you will not need keys for the car. It is computer coded for your voices only."

"You mean no one can get into this car but me and Janet?"

"No Tim, no one can *start* the car but you and Janet."

Tim looked pleased with Ahmad's work.

Howard stared at Tim longer than he should have and Tim noticed. He then tried avoiding Howard's stare.

Holloway spoke. "We added inventory in Asgedom's store. We have 150 cubic zirconiums, 10 moissanites and 2 diamonds in the display cabinets. Miami office will be securing the store 24/7. Until we sense actual action from Gregorvsky's camp, we still have to keep Miami in the loop. Two agents will be in the coffee shop across from the store. Asgedom will be meeting with Hasai and Gregorvsky today at 12:30 p.m. We anticipate they will already have a person seated at the Shark Tank Restaurant by the time Asgedom arrives."

"Good work Gil," Howard added. "Let's have Miami put a man and a woman in the restaurant – seated separately. Make sure that one arrives 10 minutes before our person does and the other arrives shortly after our person. Scope out who is already in the restaurant. If I know uncreative Gregorvsky, his person will be a man, most likely reading either the dog or horse race section of a newspaper. Look for someone eating a big lunch. He will want to be in the restaurant awhile. Have someone who can read lips nearby. We don't want Gregorvsky checking and finding a wire or firearm on Asgedom. Ahmad, where is the car?"

"In the garage, right beneath us."

"Tim, Janet, let's go check it out."

Chapter 37

Word finally reached Ichiro Hasai that Harry Dennis was dead. *The Philly P.D. will be paid handsomely for the info...as usual.* Now Hasai had to hope Gregorvsky's info was correct. A more important question crawled across his brain - *who killed Dennis?*

#

Across the Schuylkill River, a meeting of a different sort was taking place. A young woman was outlining a plan to confiscate a briefcase. Six young men all wearing jackets that read DTO (death to oppressors), gathered around her and listened intently as she outlined the strategy. She wanted them to understand that they had to get the briefcase *even if they had to kill the courier.*

One man had a question. "Should we look in the briefcase to make sure your contents are there?"

"No" she answered. "I don't care about the contents. I already know what is in the briefcase; I just want to get it off the street. Besides, the courier is so conditioned that he will never give you the keys."

"What if the courier gives up the keys with no problem?" the same man asked. "Do we still have to take care of him?"

"Yes" she answered almost coldly. "The couriers have been programmed to never give up the briefcase without a fight. We do not want a fight; we just want the briefcase. Just make sure you wear the plastic clothing, including shoes and gloves. Remember to dump the clothing in different trash receptacles miles from the scene. Does everyone understand?" Everyone nodded.

"Good. Don't forget to put the note in the pocket of the courier's clothing. I will pay you once the job is completed." She then handed out six pairs of plastic clothing wear.

"How can we be sure you won't skip out on us after we take care of this job?" another man asked.

"You can't be sure" she answered, more coldly than before. "What you must believe is that who ever told you about me must have been paid as agreed."

"You may ask a last question", she said to the group.

"Not that I don't want this job" yet another asked," but why aren't you using them again?"

"Because people get comfortable when they get familiar; then they get lazy and sloppy. Fresh bodies, no problems."

\#

Chapter 38

Patrice Asgedom was cleaning the glass cases in "his shop" when two men walked in and starting looking around as if they were waiting for others. Asgedom was the only person in the shop but he was ready. When one of the men began asking technical questions about gemstones Asgedom's flag went up and he placed his hands on the activator on his belt buckle. When pressed, the mechanism would signal the FBI agents seated in the coffee shop across the street. *Someone was about to show his hand.* Unfortunately, Asgedom quickly realized that he was wrong about the two men. They were merely looking for an engagement ring and both were nervous about their upcoming nuptials.

Miami FBI was casing the neighborhood when they spotted Gregorvsky's rented Mercedes. Another agent quickly took Asgedom's place in the shop as he hurried to the Shark Tank Restaurant.

#

Chapter 39

The black jeep pulled up in front of a three-story Greystone building. Onella Katenta glanced in several directions before getting out, and then hurried up the building's stairs to her second floor apartment. As she put her key in the lock, she heard her apartment phone ringing and rushed in to answer it. She began speaking in French.

The conversation became heated until a doorbell brought the exchange to a grinding halt. Katenta stayed on the line while ambling over to the window. She peered through the blinds to see who was buzzing her door. She did not know the Black man at the door, and therefore did not answer the buzzer. When the man glanced up at her window Katenta jumped back out of sight. *This man knows where I reside.* She murmured something to her caller, terminated the call and dialed another number. When the person on the other end picked up, she spoke in an African dialect.

She went back to the window but now the man was gone. She peered up and down the street to see if he was sitting in a vehicle. She did not see anyone sitting in a vehicle. She figured the man had pushed the wrong bell and was finally buzzed in by the correct person. Had she looked across the street however, she would have noticed binoculars pointed in her direction. ATF Agents Woods and Carlson were occupying an empty second floor apartment across the street. Carlson was observing with binoculars while Woods was monitoring sound. Carlson was also reading Katenta's lips.

Katenta finished her conversation, checked her messages and left the apartment. She got back into her jeep and drove off. Carlson and Woods followed. She drove to the same abandoned building outside of Philly. Carlson and Woods were able to stay a mile back because Carlson knew where she was headed. Katenta pulled up in front of the familiar building and went down the stairs to the basement. She did not use her key because a Black man with a French accent met her at the door and let her inside.

"What is the problem Beebo?" she asked in French.

"I am curious," he said to her in a whisper. "Did you move the briefcases to another spot?"

"No, I did not" she answered as she hurried to the basement closet."Do you think my men took them?"

"I don't know" Beebo answered. "Who else (looking around the basement) knew about your hiding place?"

"No one Beebo. It had to be my last men."

"Why?" he asked. "Why your last men?"

"Because they are the only ones who asked about my opening the briefcases. It had to be them."

"Okay, if you are certain of this I will have my men trail them for a couple of days. Do these men not realize only you and I have the keys to open them?"

"No they do not."

"Onella my dear, please be very careful on which ground to tread now. You have made new enemies."

Agents Carlson and Woods took off their headphones and stared at each other for a lengthy time. Carlson called Jergensen. "*We now have a name.*"

#

Chapter 40

Gregorvsky and Hasai walked into the Shark Tank Restaurant promptly at 12:30pm and looked around. They did not know what Asgedom looked like but they knew he would find them. Asgedom arrived at the restaurant right behind them. He waited for the maitre d to seat the men and then joined them two minutes later. They each showed their cordial sides while the waiter poured their water glasses. Once they ordered lunch, business started promptly.

"Mr. Asgedom", Gregorvsky began, I am nervous and would feel safer if you not mind a walk?"

"No of course not", Asgedom said with an African accent. Both men retreated to the men's room where Gregorvsky promptly patted down Asgedom. "You must forgive my manners Mr. Asgedom, but I have been betrayed too many times to really trust anyone."

"I understand Mr. Gregorvsky but do not let your manners interfere with disrespect again. Am I understood?"

Gregorvsky ignored the question.

The men returned to the table and Gregorvsky gave Hasai a "thumbs up" look. A woman seated in the back of the restaurant "read" every word Hasai and Gregorvsky uttered even through mouthfuls of food.

In between sips of espresso, Hasai asked, "How did you come to know about my mine Mr. Asgedom?"

Asgedom took his time answering. Looking directly into Ichiro Hasai's eyes he answered, "About three years ago I was asking questions in a little village called Kabinda and a man that goes by the name of Beebo stopped me on the street and answered my questions. He said for a small sum, he would give me names of mine owners looking for partners. I of course believed him, and here you are and so am I."

Hasai studied him for a moment as if he was sorting out the information. He then looked at Gregorvsky. "Mr. Gregorvsky don't we have a man named Baybo on our payroll?

Gregorvsky nodded. "It seems Mr. Baybo has been busy." Hasai looked back at Asgedom. "What can we do for you Mr. Asgedom?"

"I would like to invest in your company...if you have room for 300 million dollars. I have several stores in Miami, Philadelphia and of course in Addis Ababa. If not, Mr. Baybo wasted not only my time and money but your time as well." He waited a full moment before he looked directly into Hasai's eyes again. The chess piece was ready for two moves down the board.

#

The agents met later in Howard's suite to go over the day's activities. The female agent reading the lips of those at the table in the Shark Tank briefed Howard on what was said. Howard also learned that Ahmad's team had time to plant a device on Gregorvsky's car even with his protection standing in front of it smoking cigarettes.

"Okay, agents listen up. Our plant in the Congo is ready to vouch for Asgedom. Our people in Ethiopia are also sitting on the same information. We have just been informed that keeping Harry Dennis' death under wraps is no longer needed. Our cover has been compromised. Hasai must have paid handsomely for this info."

"What do you want us to do now Howard?" Tim asked.

"I want us to continue our mission. We have now found our fall guy. We need to know why a young woman is not only a thief but also might be the head of a gang who has murdered four...five men now. We need to know who she is and why she is doing what she is doing. We also need to know why she *hasn't* taken any of the contents in the briefcases even though all four cases had several diamonds in them worth over $5 million dollars."

Jergensen broke in. "We also want the complete whereabouts of Gregorvsky and Hasai. I will tell one of my men to drop a dime on old man Hasai by letting him know what Hasai the younger is doing. *Of course, he will do this subtly.*

#

Chapter 41

Juliana Forrestal put down the newspaper. The article was about a funeral in West Virginia. It referred to a former Washington, D.C. FBI agent and Vietnam veteran named Hilton Dennis who had been laid to rest. The article went on to name all the daring and courageous things Dennis had done in his life. It also mentioned the many awards both academically and militarily that he had amassed during his 58 years on earth. The article said that Hilton (called Harry to his friends) had been outgoing in college and graduate school, but his tour in Vietnam, and especially his time in a POW camp, left its scar on him, and according to close friends, he became somewhat of a recluse.

The family was surprised to find that Hilton had fathered a daughter whom they knew nothing about. They found over 150 letters written to her over a period of 30 years. Since the letters had no address, they were never mailed.

Juliana now knew Harry's whereabouts. She allowed her eyes to let go of the tears she had been holding back for 34 years. After awhile she went to her bedroom dresser and pulled out the drawer that held her jewelry box. Taped to the inside bottom of the box were two college pictures of her and Harry. She was getting ready to tape them back to the bottom when the doorbell rang. She quickly placed the pictures in the box, composed herself, went downstairs and answered the door to the women invited to her garden party.

#

Chapter 42

Janet loved the ring. She stared at it longer than she should have and garnered a chuckle from Howard. "Agent Forrestal, perhaps you should ask your Chief if you can keep the ring once this assignment is completed." Everyone in the room laughed, including Janet.

At that very moment Howard's cell phone rang. "I just received word that Gregorvsky is on his way to the shop so everyone get suited up."

All of the agents in the room dispersed like ants. Howard looked at Bruce Jergensen and said, "Here we go."

Janet and Tim drove the rental car to Asgedom's shop and amazingly entered before Gregorvsky had gotten there. Janet knew what Gregorvsky looked like but still a little nervous when she actually saw him enter the store with another man in tow. She motioned to Tim who took his cue immediately. Both started speaking in Japanese. Gregorvsky looked over at the unusual couple, one a woman, surely mixed, and the other a dark Asian man, both speaking Japanese. He noticed the most spectacular diamond he had ever seen on her finger. He was intrigued. He inquired about it with Asgedom who said he was the seller.

"Is there some place we can speak with no interruption?

"What do you wish to speak about?" was all Asgedom could muster up once he and Gregorvsky walked into the back room.

"I would like to ask if you know where that diamond came from. I mean what country?"

"I get all my diamonds from Kabinda, a little village in the DRC." Asgedom felt confident of the next question. "DRC?" Gregorvsky asked. "Democratic Republic of the Congo" Asgedom answered. He knew the next question too.

"Do you know this for sure? Were you actually told where the diamonds are from?"

"Why are you asking me these questions sir? Asgedom asked. "The reason I am asking," Gregorvsky sputtered, "is because the ladies' diamond is so brilliant, so beautifully shaped and the setting is exceptional. Did you do this?"

"Actually no", Asgedom answered. "The Associate I spoke of Mr. Beebo, had a master jeweler carve out the rock for Ms. Davenport."

"Can I ask the name of this master who obviously knows exquisite quality?" Gregorvsky inquired as casually as he could.

I thought you'd never ask. "I should get his card for you," Asgedom answered. "His name is Jeremiah".

As Gregorvsky walked back into the show room, he asked one last question. "Would your three hundred million be in cash?"

Asgedom nodded.

#

Chapter 43

Koriuko Hasai uncharacteristically slumped down on the sofa in his office. He tried to soak in the information the man was telling him without getting ill. "Are you sure it is my son?" he asked the man. "Are you telling me he has a business on the side that he is not telling me about but using my money to fund it?" The man nodded his head and showed him the many pictures of Hasai in and around the Congolese diamond mine.

"Your son is working with a Russian named Nikola Gregorvsky. In a trade off situation, Ichiro's company mines the diamonds and then barters with Gregorvsky for stainless steel. This is how you are able to produce your steel relatively cheaply. With the diamonds from your son's mine Gregorvsky purchases weapons and sells them to various African and Russian factions bent on revolt."

Koriuko looked directly at the man and asked, "What is it that you want from me?"

"All I want is a part of the action. Your son is having security problems with his mine in the Congo. I can guarantee better security efforts for three years. Your son cannot afford to keep the peace in the Congo without someone who knows the country and region well. If you want to think about it, I can surely wait…but not long. If you do not want my assistance I will go away and be no further bother."

Koriuko looked beaten. "How do I know you are being truthful? How do I know the government doesn't already know this?"

The man smiled. "You don't know. He handed Koriuko a piece of paper. "This is my number. Have your son call me if he is interested." Agent Carlson walked away.

Agent Woods adjusted his earpiece and smiled behind binoculars. He immediately placed his call.

"Agent Jergensen, Woods reporting in."

"What ya got Woods" Bruce replied.

"Sir, Pearl Harbor has been bombed." Woods then hung up.

\#

Chapter 44

Janet and Tim were slightly disappointed when they found out that the camera installed on their car did not single out any particular car that might have been following them. They basked in the notion that at least the camera worked. Janet stared at the ring on her finger probably longer than she should have and Tim noticed. She felt as if she should have been embarrassed but interestingly she was not.

She had hoped Gregorvsky would have talked to her or at least approached "her fiancé" in the store but he did neither.

She had a feeling the Russian would return to the store the next day. She was right. Gregorvsky and another man returned the next afternoon and inquired again about Janet's ring. He wanted to know exactly where he could find the same elaborate stone for his mistress. Asgedom chuckled and mentioned to Gregorvsky that he was in luck as Ms. Davenport and her fiancé were due shortly to have the ring re-sized. Gregorvsky looked pleased and busied himself in the store by perusing other gems in the display cases. For such a small store, he found several stones to be of unbelievable quality. He made a phone call.

"I am in small store with big gems. Wondering if you heard name of Asgedom?" The voice on the other end was succinct. "No" was all he said. Gregorvsky added, "Find out about him and report to me later." He then hung up as Janet and Tim entered the store.

Asgedom introduced Tim and Janet to Gregorvsky. He also mentioned that Gregorvsky was intrigued by the beauty and quality of her ring. Janet nervously showed it to him. Gregorvsky more than looked at it - he studied it. "I see you have fabulous taste Mrs....."

"Ms. Davenport" Janet said through a smile. Looking in Tim's direction, she interpreted in Japanese that the man admired her ring. Tim looked at Gregorvsky and nodded. Gregorvsky then asked Asgedom if his master jeweler was in the store. Asgedom nodded. "He is usually here cn Thursdays to resize, reshape, sign certificates, those sorts of things. This is why Ms. Davenport and her fiancé Mr. Hayashi are here today."

Janet and Tim did not see Gregorvsky's companion taking pictures of her ring. Nor did they see him take pictures of Asgedom.

Asgedom then introduced Gregorvsky to his "master jeweler" Jeremiah - a young agent from the Miami FBI office who took a crash course in Dr. Denny's lab.

For the next 15 minutes Gregorvsky asked the young man everything under the sun – from whom did he learn his technique, to where did he hone his skills to craft such exquisite stones, to what does he charge? The young man's performance was impeccable. He also mentioned that he had been schooled by a man named Julius Beebo in Philadelphia. He was way ahead of the curve because Gil Holloway and Ahmad Waverly had schooled *him* on delivering his lines. Later Dr. Denny would be proud.

#

Chapter 45

After an exhausting day, Howard caught up with Tim and requested they talk later in his room. Tim had no idea they would be talking personally.

"What's going on with you?" Howard began. "Is it Kelly? Is she all right? Do you need more time at home? If so, you got it."

Tim started loosening his tie while taking his time answering. He walked over to the wet bar and made himself a drink. He took a sip. "Howard, did you really want kids? I mean for real. I know Mark is the greatest kid in the world, but did you really want kids? How do you juggle work and home and kids and…life?"

Howard had known Tim for almost 15 years but was floored by the questions. He hadn't realized that the "baby request" had come up again. "Kelly's talking about wanting kids again?"

"Yeah Howard. This time I really don't know what to do. This subject has been making us drift apart for the past two years but now I have the feeling the boat has sailed.

I don't think I can hurt her anymore. I truly believe the miscarriage was an omen."

"Maybe…I don't know Tim. I remember before I met Carol and Mark I was always on the go wherever, anywhere that this job took me. I was 36, no kids, no wife, only this job. Don't get me wrong, I love this job, but Tim it is only *part* of my life. Carol and Mark were the gift from another man…my buddy. I hope he's smiling right now from the irony."

"What do you mean irony Howard?"

"I mean you remember John. He was a great guy. He was my friend and my buddy. You also remember he was murdered. He told Carol and Mark that if anything were to happen to him that they had to get to *me*…remember? He believed I would save them. The irony Tim is that they saved *me*.

"What do you mean saved you?"

"I mean I was a skeleton. I had nothing on my bones but myself. My parents, God bless them, were, and are the best role models around. I was finally at the age in which I really wanted more in my life that I could come home to…as my father did. Shit Tim, my mother is a saint! (Laughter). Where was I going to find that kind of woman? Nowhere!"

"That's what I thought until Carol and Mark came into my life and plopped down on my heart. I couldn't fight it… didn't want to." The room was silent for several moments.

"Look, marriage isn't for everyone and certainly kids are a major step but I'm happy with three boys running in opposite directions – all of them smart, athletic, good kids. My parents are still alive and vibrant. My sisters and their husbands have their own lives and not living off my parents or me. Best of all? My wife is wonderful. I truly thank God for all of this life. You…you gotta do what floats your boat. Whatever it is, I'm here."

Before Tim had an opportunity to completely absorb the good advice, a knock sounded at the door. It was Gil Holloway.

"I wanted you to know that Gregorvsky is traveling. He's probably on his way to pay a visit to Mr. Beebo. We need to get to him before Gregorvsky does."

Howard started dialing. "Don't say my name. The bird has flown the coop!"

Agent Woods responded, "Yes sir, on our way."

#

Chapter 46

Koriuko Hasai was furious. Ichiro could see it on his face as he entered through the doors of his father's mansion.

"What is the meaning" he yelled at Ichiro, "of your going behind my back and committing these atrocities?" You will not under any circumstances disgrace what I have builit in America. You have now shamed this family and our name!"

Ichiro looked squarely at his father. "I have made things better Father. You were thinking too small. In addition, do not forget I am the one who made this company larger and more profitable. We now have monies for your grandchildren and their children. With our additional investments in Africa, you no longer have to worry about the Hasai name being erased from the minds of the patrons ever."

"Is this what you think I came to America for? To plant brainwash? I came to America to get away from brainwash! Do you realize that you are hurting and killing children and families in another land because you are greedy? My parents and their parents only wanted the best for me and it had nothing…you hear me…nothing to do with money! It was about honor, and integrity, and respect and our reputation! You must give up this business in Africa or else you leave me no choice but to change my will."

"I'm sorry Father that you feel this way," Ichiro said turning his back on his father. "The family had decided months ago that you needed a rest because you seem to be slipping with your memory. My attorney and I took a look at your will and to protect you from certain dangers changed the name of your Executor to reflect my attorney's name."

"You cannot do this Ichiro!"

"Oh but I can Father, and did. Your leadership has been spotty for the past five years and you have not been on the operations side in the past 10 years. You are simply a figurehead. Do not worry Father I have your and mother's best interest at heart. Do not worry, my brothers will never want for anything either. I have the greatest love and respect for you and mother. The Board of Directors have each received your letter of retirement as President and CEO and naming me as your successor. I will be heading up Hasai Auto Parts and Hasai Manufacturing now."

Koriuko screamed at his son, "You are a disgrace and I cannot look at you anymore. Go!"

Ichiro started to say more but decided against it. He left in a huff.

Koriuko sat on the sofa in the foyer of his house, looked around and placed his head in his hands.

His wife heard every word from the second level of the spiral staircase.

#

Chapter 47

Julius Beebo had just gotten off the SEPTA train and was walking to his loft apartment just outside the Center City area when two men asked him to accompany them to a meeting. In this business, Beebo was used to these late night meetings - this was just another one. Before they frisked him, he had put three numbers in his cell phone and put it in his vest pocket. The men found no gun on him but confiscated his wallet and cell phone. After 15 minutes in the backseat of the sedan, he finally asked where they were headed? The two men seemed to ignore his question so Beebo asked again. The man in the front passenger seat turned around, pointed a gun in Beebo's face and said, "We are instructed to deliver you to meet with Mr. Gregorvsky... willingly if possible." The car doors were locked.

Beebo was shocked. What could he have possibly done to warrant such behavior? *Maybe it has something to do with Onella.*

The car pulled up in front of a dilapidated garage in an area full of boarded up buildings desperately waiting for City inspectors to condemn them. This made Beebo nervous. The two men in the front seat got out of the car and one opened the door for Beebo. They walked alongside him into the garage where Ichiro Hasai's First Lieutenant was waiting.

"Mr. Beebo, how are things going with you?" the henchman asked. Beebo was then provided a chair, complete with ropes. The two men who had escorted him to the garage tied both his feet and hands to the chair. Afterwards they took their place alongside two other men working for the henchman. Beebo looked at the henchman. "What is going on here?" he asked.

"Mr. Beebo, does not Mr. Gregorvsky pay you a handsome salary to watch over his assets?" he asked.

Beebo look confused. "Why yes, of course he does. What is the meaning of all of this cloak and dagger stuff? I demand to know!"

"Mr. Beebo, Mr. Gregorvsky has come to the conclusion that you are stealing from him and he wants to know before we cut off your hand…why?"

Two hundred yards away in an abandoned church tower, others were listening in on the exchange. Agent Woods turned to Carlson. "We probably need someone to tell us our next step here because this is about to get ugly." Carlson started dialing.

A hundred yards in another direction, two DEA agents were listening in on the same dialogue on the third floor of a boarded-up Greystone apartment building. One asked, "What's our next move?" The other took a pause. "Let's see what Woods and Carlson are going to do first. We won't let Beebo lose any limbs if that's your concern."

#

"Agent Carlson", Bruce began, "move in when you think the moment has come when Beebo's accusers will not take "no" for an answer. He looked at Howard who nodded in agreement across the room on the other phone.

"Roger, Agent Jergensen."

After hanging up with Jergensen, Carlson glanced around the church tower and spied several empty beer cans, an empty bottle of Crown Royal and some filthy clothes. He started taking off his clothes. Woods looked at him incredulously. "What are you doing?" he asked. "Going in" he said. "But definitely back me up."

Carlson moaned when he picked up the clothing. "These probably belong to the guy who lives here". He then held his breath as he put on the clothes. He placed the two empty beer cans in the pockets of the jacket. The empty bottle of Crown he carried with him. He looked back at Woods as he descended the tower stairs and said, "Pay attention because you'll know the moment I'm gonna need you. Lock and load."

The DEA agent's phone was vibrating; it was Howard. "Roger, Agent Jergensen" was all he said before ending the call. "This is going to go down fast," he said to the other agent. He then led him to a boarded up window and pulled off a thin slat so they could see what would be happening in the next few minutes. "There he is," he said pointing. Both men looked down at the street and saw Agent Carlson bend down, put some murky street water into a Crown Royal bottle and stagger in a drunkenly way to the garage.

Two more eyes were watching the picture develop. These eyes were black and slanted.

#

Chapter 48

Onella Katenta paced back and forth in her living room. *Where is Beebo? He should have called by now.* She picked up her cell phone, started dialing but quickly stopped. She started dialing again, but stopped again. She started pacing again. Her apartment phone rang. She glanced at the number and picked up the receiver. She started speaking in French. The caller said he had found Beebo's location. "Merci, merci" she said happily and hung up. She took a deep breath and made a phone call on her cell phone. This time she spoke in Ibinda, an African dialect. Afterwards she grabbed her purse, fled down the stairs, and jumped in her Jeep. She then sped away.

Two CIA OPS followed her on GPS.

#

Even through a mouthful of blood, Beebo still maintained his innocence. "I have not stolen from anyone", he said repeatedly to the thugs beating him.

"Mr. Beebo," the henchman countered, "if you would just say that you have stolen from Mr. Gregorvsky and tell us where you have deposited the money you will only have to lose one hand. But, if you continue to maintain that you are innocent, we will have to take more than one hand... perhaps even an eye?"

Still Beebo maintained his innocence.

At that moment four vehicles, one a black Jeep, crashed through the closed garage doors taking the gathered by surprise. Eight people wearing masks and carrying 9mm Berettas surrounded the men inside. The henchman was the first to go. The other four men dropped to their knees and put their hands behind their heads thinking they would eventually be set free. Three of them were wrong. The fourth would be the only one to relay what happened...once he got out of the hospital.

By the time the ATF, DEA and CIA agents reached the garage the vehicles had blazed a trail hard to follow. They had also taken Julius Beebo with them.

Agent Carlson sat down on the fire hydrant outside the garage he was going to enter and waited for the various OPS to give him answers to what had just happened.

#

"What?" was all Bruce could ask. "What happened?" he asked again.

"Sir", Carlson explained, "As we were about to move in, four vehicles, including a black Jeep, blazed into the garage, knocking out the doors. After hearing what we now know were gunshots, we saw two men drag a bleeding and seemingly unconscious Julius Beebo out and place him in the black Jeep, which sped away immediately. The other vehicles left almost as fast. We really had no time to follow sir."

"Carlson, do you think Onella Katenta was the driver of the Jeep?"

"Yes sir, I think she was sir."

"Do you know if Agent Woods got any plates?"

"Sir, I believe Agent Woods can identify Onella Katenta as the driver of the black Jeep."

"Carlson, you and Woods have this report to me by email this evening. I'll wait to hear from DEA to see what they got, if anything."

"Yes sir, Agent Jergensen."

Howard had also been listening on the speakerphone and could only purse his lips to ask Bruce "what the hell is going on?"

"I don't know Howard, but I bet Onella Katenta knows. We need CIA to give us everything on her."

#

Chapter 49

The newspapers reported the following:
Four dead in apparent gangland shooting

"Four men were shot to death in an abandoned garage in the lower eastside neighborhood of Dunkirk, just outside Philadelphia city limits. A fifth man, police say, is currently listed in critical condition in Ben Franklin County Hospital and armed police are guarding his ICU room. Police have not given out any names at this time pending notice to family. The garage, owned by Framingham Sheet Metal, a company repeatedly charged with flagrant building violations and whose owners are still being sought by several government entities, including OSHA, could not be reached for their response to this incident. The property, formerly owned by Hasai Manufacturing Company, was sold to Framingham in the early 80's. The police have no further details at this time."

#

Ichiro Hasai was livid. *Who could have possibly given our name to this?*

"Gregorvsky...

...the source of my disturbance."

He should not have trusted the Russian. Gregorvsky was the person who told him about Asgedom. Asgedom gave them Beebo's name. *Who is Asgedom?* He dialed a number. "Find out everything about Patrice Asgedom. I must know everything about him. I need this today!"

The voice at the other end said one word, "okay".

He then sent a text asking, "who are Cassandra Davenport and William Hayashi; where did they get a five carat flawless diamond and not come through us?"

Twenty minutes later, he received several answers that did not sit well with him.

#

Chapter 50

When he heard the news on the phone Stanton Abrams dropped his unlit cigar in his lap. "Come again?" he asked Bruce.

"Sorry Stanton" Bruce said almost apologetically. "That's what went down. Right now, we'd like you to issue a directive to CIA to flag a young woman named Onella Katenta. Based on her name she might be from France or Haiti, or maybe Senegal. She speaks fluent French. She is a major piece of this puzzle."

"Why do you believe that Bruce? Where is Howard? Is he on this call?"

"Yes Stanton, I'm on the call. Bruce and I think without a doubt that Katenta's strategy is to divide Hasai and Gregorvsky. For some reason or reasons we are unaware, this seems personal."

"Why do you say that?"

"Can't give you a specific answer yet, but this theory fits better than most at this time. Stanton, we also need CIA to check if the Hasai's have any manufacturing plants in Oaxaca, Mexico. We came up with what we believe might be a zip code from Russian chatter in some limited correspondence."

"Okay you can explain all of this to me when I get to Miami tomorrow. In the meantime, I will need reports from your people. Is this understood?"

Both men said yes.

"Also both of you gather all involved for a meeting tomorrow at 1400 hours in the conference suite of my hotel." He hung up.

Howard dialed Carol to tell her he would be in Miami for at least several more days. "I understand Howard" was all she said. Howard read between the lines – "I know this is your job, but sometimes it sucks".

#

Tim and Janet were drinking on the veranda of their apartment when they each received a call announcing a scheduled meeting for 7 p.m. in Howard's room at the hotel. Janet looked at her watch recognizing that they had three hours to prepare.

"Janet" Tim said without looking at her. "Could you give me some elbow room so that I can talk to my wife without my screaming getting on your nerves?"

"Sure Tim, I was going to my room anyway to look over our notes. If you need me, call me…I mean it." She then picked up her drink, turned in the direction of her room and walked away. Tim stared at her for a pregnant moment and then dialed Kelly…who answered almost immediately.

The conversation seemed strained, almost exhausting. Tim remembered when it was fun to talk to her on the phone, from the road, from the office or from the corner store. Kelly always unloaded loads of information from her day. It was great exchanging stories. Although he couldn't divulge specifics, it was always stimulating talking war stories with her.

What has happened to us? I haven't seen her smile in a long time. Maybe she is tired too.

"Tim," she said before they hung up, "I think we should maybe take a break."

It hit Tim like a load of bricks. "What do you mean by taking a break Kelly?"

"I mean going in other directions that will make us both happy. This marriage obviously isn't working for you and…"

He cut her off. "You really want this?"

"Yes Tim, I really want this."

"I should be back in D.C. soon and I think we should talk about this before, you know, we do something we might regret."

"Tim, I'm sorry but I have already made up my mind. When you get back we can start on legal separation or divorce, whichever you choose."

"Kelly…"

"Tim, I've gotta go. Take care." She quickly hung up the phone, plopped down on the sofa and cried.

Janet was returning her empty glass to the kitchen sink when she saw Tim staring at the phone in his hand.

"Janet, she wants a divorce."

Janet kept the smile to herself.

#

Chapter 51

"Agents", Stanton Abrams began. "I want to talk about these last two weeks and specifically piece together just what happened this afternoon in Philadelphia. I have ATF on the line. Agents Carlson and Woods, can you hear me?"

Both said, "We hear you" in unison.

"What about you Keaton?" You on?"

"OPS reporting Stanton."

"Okay agents, we have Holloway, Forrestal, Yamamoto, Waverly and Supervising Agents Watson, Jergensen and me here in the room. We want to start with the earliest report and then we can move to the next phase. Woods, let's begin with you and Carlson."

Woods: **"About a month ago, Agent Carlson and I were tailing a black 2002 Jeep Cherokee because we had been given information earlier in the week that a vehicle fitting the Jeep's description had been seen leaving an alley in the City Center area of Philly only moments before someone found the second** courier's body. Although our witnesses did not get a license plate number, they did give us a description of the vehicle and the woman driver.

Of course, we banished any thought of coincidence. We knew this had to be the same woman.

We worked the neighborhoods until we found several of our "neighborhood watch" people willing to give up information on the vehicle, specifically where it is most nights, that they've heard the driver speak several languages, etc. Two nights later, we found the vehicle parked behind a Greystone building in the Museum area of the city. That night we were able to attach, without detection, monitoring devices on the inside front wheels of the Jeep.

The next morning we arrived at the site at six hundred hours and waited to see who would come and claim the vehicle. We only had to wait an hour. We followed the vehicle to a blighted area about five miles outside the city limits. We stayed at least eight car lengths behind. Agent Carlson and I put on utility workers clothing, scaled up the highest pole we could find, and through our binoculars watch the woman driver get out of the vehicle followed by three men passengers. The woman was carrying what we now know is the latest courier's briefcase. She went down several basement steps located in the front of the building and let herself in with a key. Less than 10 minutes later, the woman returned to the Jeep without the briefcase. The three male passengers followed suit.

Once the Jeep was clearly out of sight, Woods and I descended the utility pole, ran through the high grasses and bushes and slipped behind the building. Although the Greystone was completely boarded-up, we were able to find several boards missing in the kitchen window located in the very back of the building. We climbed through and searched the basement first where we saw empty crates and boxes but nothing else. We were on our way to the second floor when we noticed a cell phone vibrating on the kitchen counter. We quickly realized the owner would be returning for it. We were right, and just in time too as we heard a vehicle pull up in front of the building. Woods and I hid in the broom closet and could hear two males talking. The owner of the cell phone was one of the woman driver's cohorts as they referred to her in their conversation. We stayed hidden until they left. We then called Agent Watson for more instructions.

After talking with Agent Watson, we went back in and searched the basement again, this time finding a door behind the crates and boxes we missed the first time. The door opened to some sort of closet that was empty except for five stainless steel briefcases on the floors. We quickly reported our findings to

Special Agent Watson and turned our bounty over to the ATF.

I'm done."

"Thank you Agent Woods" Abrams said chomping on his cigar. "Fine job. Bruce I'd like you to share a copy of this report with our Agency by 0800 hours tomorrow if you can make this possible."

"I'm sure we can make this possible sir" Jergensen replied.

"We'd like a copy too" Keaton piped in."

"You'll not be left out of the loop Rick." Stanton said dryly. "Holloway, you're up."

Holloway: "**Agent Forrestal and I have been working this particular detail for the past 22, almost 23 months since the first courier's body was discovered under the bridge in the Diamond District. The reason we were given the detail was because Chief of Police Samuelson was/is under the belief that some of his police officers might be working part-time for a splinter group that could include diamond smuggling into the U.S. Agent Forrestal and I shared the unpleasant task of tagging the toe of the first four courier victims. Although Samuelson didn't want to ruffle any feathers in case he was wrong, he also didn't want the word to escape that he had Internal Affairs looking into this matter. After I.A. confirmed that the splinter group existed, Samuelson contacted our superior to make sure all information we were working on stayed out of the hands of those who might be rogue cops. We made sure no Philadelphia cop had any knowledge that the last body we tagged was an** ex-FBI agent. We are thinking someone in the M.E's office must have been paid handsomely for divulging the information.

After our second victim was found, Forrestal and I were given information by a couple of jewelers who were, in the beginning, reluctant to give up info on their supplier. We finally wrestled the details out of them. It seems that unhappiness is creeping into the gem community. The jewelers are being forced to purchase various gems with signatures on the certs that they don't recognize as part of the "79 diamond families". When one of the jewelers sought more specifics on the unfamiliar names, according to him, he was told to "stand back". We asked what this meant and the jeweler said, "don't cause trouble". This particular jeweler said the supplier worked for a man named Nikola Gregorvsky.

That's it for me sir."

"Good job Agent Holloway. You and Forrestal have this report to me by 0800 hours. Is this clear?"

Both Janet and Gil answered "yes sir!"

Keaton does the CIA have a report they're willing to share?"

Keaton: "Stanton, our people have been following Julius Beebo for the past 18 months mostly because he works for Nikola Gregorvsky and manufacturing magnate Ichiro Hasai. He is their intermediary for Hasai's Seigo-sei Mining Company in DRC. Beebo arranges for the kimberlite rocks that come out of Hasai's mine to be cleaned up for sale, usually in a western country because the people in the DRC don't have the capability of cutting and finishing rough diamonds. So, most exporting is handled by third party countries – like Belgium. Once the gems are ready for distribution Beebo connects somehow with the gemology society, (whom we're sure don't know where these diamonds are really headed) and they certify the gems. Afterwards, Hasai and Gregorvsky connect with the Africans and divvy up the spoils, "allowing" the DRC to take their share off the top. Hasai hands over some of the diamonds to Gregorvsky whose people sell them all over the globe.

Gregorvsky sends some of his money to Russia, Norilsk to be exact, where the nickel is produced. Gregorvsky's people then ship tons of the converted nickel to Hasai's manufacturing plants in Jersey, Pennsylvania and New York.

The balance of the money goes to various African warlords who meet them in Norilsk. These insurgents buy guns, ammunition *and* heads of state with the money from the protection racket they got going by keeping the diamond mining equipment and transportation vehicles safe and unharmed. The warlords then use these weapons to become the next so-called leaders of their new socialist regimes.

Some, like Julius Beebo get diamond samples

from the mine owners and give them to couriers, who then come to the U.S. to sell to the various wholesale jewelers. Right now, the mine owners think Beebo is skimming because now five shipments have not made it to the jewelers for sale.

We have a theory. We have been tracking a young woman named Onella Katenta. Although from Africa, the DRC to be specific, she attended a prestigious university in North West central France called *Superior Institute of Trades*. As a student, she wanted to find out everything possible on delivering dairy products to her people in her little village. She is very smart. She speaks several languages and while in college assisted on a progressive study of producing ultra high temperature processing of milk. According to fellow students, she wanted to return home full of complete knowledge and as an authority in the dairy industry, which barely exists. Somewhere along this path, something went awry. We don't quite know what...yet, but we will and when we do, we'll let you know. Katenta is not at all interested in the briefcases or what they contain, so we need to know how she finds out about the couriers. We know that she and Julius Beebo are associates so it doesn't make sense that she is stabbing him in the back by hiring thugs to take care of those couriers. Right now, it's supposed to look as if Beebo is behind the rash of thefts but our people say he is not. Regardless, Katenta is adamant about couriers not making it to their destination so we have devised a plan. We have a decoy arriving in a few days in Philadelphia with less than genuine stones in a briefcase we borrowed from you people. We believe Katenta and her splinter group will find out about him. We'll be there when she does.

Last thing Stanton. Those numbers 68024 that Howard and Bruce gave us?"

"Yeah?"

"It checks out that this zip code is in a resort town in Mexico called Oaxaca. Thus far, no business of any kind is taking place that even remotely relates to this case. *However*, 68024 is also the first six numbers of geographic coordinates for Ichiro Hasai's diamond mine in Kabinda, Democratic Republic of Congo... the birthplace of Onella Katenta."

#

Chapter 52

When Nikola Gregorvsky heard about the hit on his people in the garage, he knew it was Hasai. *"That Jap wants me out of this picture. He wants to start a war; I'll give him a war. I should not have trusted him."* He started dialing.

"Do not say word. Meet at 68024 and take care of business." The voice at the other end said simply "okay."

Agent Woods called Jergensen. "Sir" he said. "Carlson and I remember a burned out warehouse in which Hasai and Gregorvsky met once. We know they swapped inventories but we didn't see it, only heard the exchange going on. It was on a dead end street that ended at a railroad yard. Should we stay close and see what happens?"

"Yes Woods, stay close, understand? I want to hear from you every 10 minutes. Understand?"

Woods understood. He imparted the news to Carlson. They got in the gray SUV, drove to the "no outlet" street, and parked blocks away. They ducked behind several empty railroad cars and waited to see if Gregorvsky's men would appear. They didn't have to wait long. A black late model Cadillac drove up to the warehouse garage doors and one door lifted. Two other black Cadillac's were already inside. Four men got out of each vehicle.

One of Gregorvsky's men manually pulled down the garage door. Woods and Carlson ran through the trees to get better reception on their earpieces. They crouched down behind a large tree. That's when they heard the click of a gun behind them.

#

Jergensen was nervous. He hadn't heard from Woods or Carlson in over 20 minutes. They didn't answer his texts. He gathered the troops. "Be careful. I don't want any agents killed. Find them; bring them home."

Howard called Philadelphia FBI office and alerted them to the location as well.

#

Chapter 53

Asgedom called Tim and Janet to the shop. "Hurry" was all he texted. Tim notified Howard and Jergensen as he and Janet got in their car and drove to the store. Before they went into the shop, they drove around the block to check for any unusual activity. They could see none that raised an eyebrow. They did see a vehicle the first time around in the retail parking lot with a driver in the front seat who looked like he was reading. The second time around he seemed to be viewing the shop. He looked Asian. Janet texted Howard and delivered the information.

The shop was empty save one man and woman looking at gems in a corner display cabinet. Asgedom did not look up but was busy texting Tim on his phone. Tim's phone vibrated in his upper jacket pocket. He stepped over to a display cabinet and slipped his phone out of his pocket to read "Gregorvsky n bk rm lkng at gms. Tlk in Jap til u lv store."

As Tim placed his phone back in his pocket, he started talking to Janet in Japanese. She quickly got the message.

Gregorvsky emerged from the backroom when he heard the Japanese conversation.

"It is good to see you Ms. Davenport and Mr. Hayashi. Perhaps you would be so kind as to tell me how your ring is now fitting. "

Janet took a pause. "It is fitting very fine now Mr.?"

"Gregorvsky. But I suspect you already know my name."

Janet and Tim looked puzzled, as did Asgedom. In that instant Tim knew what was happening. Before he could remove his gun from his ankle, four of Gregorvsky's men had entered the room with guns pointed at the three of them. They immediately seized all three agents' guns. The couple looking at gems in the corner display sized up the possible gang rivalry and left quickly. Halfway down the block the man called the police. The kidnappers quickly *escorted* the three agents to a waiting vehicle in the parking lot behind the store.

One of the kidnappers went back into the store and locked the front door. This piqued the interest of the Asian man parked in the last row in the parking lot. Janet was forced into the driver's seat of her and Tim's car because Gregorvsky quickly realized the car would only start for them. Janet drove off with a gun to her neck. Tim and Asgedom were blindfolded and shoved into another vehicle.

The Asian man watched from his car.

PART 3

"You two wanna get up?" the man said with his shotgun pointed at Carlson's head. He followed with "throw your guns on the ground and don't try anything stupid". Both Woods and Carlson stood up and threw their guns away from their bodies. "Put your hands behind your heads". They followed orders. The man then pulled a pair of handcuffs from his camouflaged jacket and told Carlson to put his hand in one, and Woods to put his hand in the other; they did what they were told. With the gun still at Carlson's head, the man pushed them to an abandoned railroad car and with another pair of handcuffs cuffed Woods' free hand to a rail car door.

"If you don't say a word, I won't say a word", he said to them as he ran through the brush. Woods look incredulously at Carlson. "What the hell just happened?" he asked. Before Carlson could even think about an answer, the man was back.

"Okay, looks like 10, maybe 12 men inside. All strapped with 9mm Berettas. They're probably drug dealers. What do you want to do, shoot and then ask questions?"

Carlson had to ask. "Who are you?" "I'm Benny Lockett," he said. "This is my land and these pond scum assholes are trying to do some type of drug deal here. At first, I thought you two were with them but I see you ain't nothing like them. What are you, the Feds?" He threw keys to both men who quickly unlocked their cuffs.

Woods suddenly realized they had a nutcase on their hands. Both agents had to decide quickly on what to do next: wait for backup or take a chance and try to make a major bust on the men in the garage.

There was that other thought – forge ahead with Benny Lockett, probably a Vietnam veteran who didn't know he was dead. Hard decision but they chose Benny…who of course had several rounds of ammunition on him. Woods explained to Benny that they could not take him into the warehouse but if he would watch for other law enforcement and let them know what was going on, he and Carlson would be most grateful. Benny thought about the task for a long moment. Finally, he said, "Okay if you're not out in ten I have to come in for you. We never leave a soldier on the battlefield…never."

Carlson called for assistance. Jergensen was somewhat relieved. "Who is this guy with you?" he asked. Carlson gave him Benny's name and said, "He would be more harmful to us or himself if he isn't with us. We *have* to use him. If for nothing else, a lookout man. Benny can do this."

Jergensen was not happy…not happy at all. "You know we can't use a civilian in an operation. No, we cannot do this Agent Carlson. We have to come up with some other plan."

"Sir" Carlson explained. "Benny will be a lookout only. He'll wait for our people and Agent Watson's men, sir. Woods and I have to make sure the pond scum as Benny called them don't leave. Sir, understand this, Benny looks Vietnam era so we are almost certain that he won't go away quietly."

#

Chapter 55

Tim and Asgedom were still blindfolded when they were led into a darkened room. Janet was already there. Although their blindfolds were removed, their hands were still cuffed behind them, as were hers. There was a sliver of light coming from the tops of the dirty windows above them. "Tim", Asgedom asked. "Take off my left shoe and slide open the heel". Both men sat on the floor so that Tim could remove Asgedom's shoe. "Now" Asgedom continued, "just press any two buttons on the heel – any two, and my coordinates will be activated."

Before Tim could do this, two of Gregorvsky's men entered the room and turned on the lights. They looked at the shoe in Tim's hand and sizing up the situation removed all three agents' shoes. After this, they frisked them, taking their time with Janet. Tim and Asgedom had to bite their tongues in order to refrain from any hint of emotion. Janet stood her ground. For the short time the lights were on Tim could see trees and the tops of bushes through the windows so he reasoned that they were in the basement of a building.

When the men left, Janet remembered her ring and asked Tim to remove the stone from the setting and then quickly replace it. When Tim did this the GPS was activated, alerting Ahmad Waverly and letting him know they were in trouble and their location.

Other trouble came fast because Janet had to go to the bathroom. The agents yelled and yelled for someone to come to the locked room, but to no avail. Asgedom spoke up. "Agent Forrestal, we don't know how long we will be detained here or if we will die here. I don't know about Tim but I will be joining you in this function soon so don't be embarrassed."

"Asgedom", Janet asked "what is your real name?"

"It's Knox Agent Forrestal; Allen Knox." At that moment, he and Tim turned their heads to allow Janet some privacy to pee in the corner of the room.

#

Chapter 56

"Howard…Tim and Janet are in trouble" was all Ahmad said.

Howard had already been alerted because someone had notified the Miami FBI. He and Keaton were relieved that Janet had activated her ring but very uncomfortable with the fact that their people had been captured.

Jergensen was feeling the same way about his men in Philadelphia. *Who is this person that is supposedly helping Carlson and Woods?*

The news came quickly.

"Benny Lockett was an Army Private in Vietnam in 1968. He was assigned to the *Charlie Company* during the My Lai Massacre and was one of the few soldiers who refused to round up and shoot civilians. Although he pleaded innocent throughout his trial, he was still detained at Ft. Benning, Georgia for more than five months because he refused to name any names."

"He was set free because other soldiers supported his story that he had nothing to do with the Massacre. Unfortunately, due to the stress of, or because of Vietnam

he became a junkie, blaming his emotional demise on the U.S. government. He sued the government and eleven years later won his case at the Supreme Court level. "

"He bought some land but no one knows what he did with the majority of the money he was awarded. He hates the government but hates drug dealers more…if there is room. No known address but he appears intermittently at several firing ranges."

Jergensen was beside himself. He started pacing back and forth. Howard finally spoke up. "We'll get them out safely Bruce. We'll get them out." Jergensen looked at Howard and tried his best to believe him.

#

Chapter 57

"Benny, you can't come. You have to stay and help our officers when they get here. Can you do this?" Carlson asked. "Yeah, I can do this" Lockett said reluctantly. "But you heard me, ten minutes is all you get." He then dashed into the brush.

With guns locked and loaded Woods and Carlson crept into the weeds and bushes, trying hard not to step on any dry branches and leaves, pine needles or garbage. They were within feet of the warehouse when they heard Benny say to them "There's twelve of them. I can take six if you two can handle the other six." Carlson groaned and looked at Woods, who gave him a look of resignation. "Okay Benny, just stay behind us, is that clear?" Carlson whispered loudly. "Yes sir!" Lockett exclaimed.

Woods, Carlson and Lockett crept along one side of the warehouse and Carlson peered into a broken window. He was able to hear and see the men standing and talking in a circle. All had guns either strapped to their chest or hanging from their side. "They're all packin'," he whispered to the others. "Also, they're opening up crates and they...are...taking guns out of the crates."

"How many crates?" Woods asked. "About eight of them" he answered. All of a sudden, three black cars drove up slowly, turning off their engines at the end of the road. Woods and Carlson believing it was their backup started to breathe a sigh of relief until they realized the six men jumping out of the vehicles were all Asian and running silently toward the warehouse. A gang war was about to take place and Woods, Carlson and Lockett had front row seats.

The Asians ran into the warehouse and all that was heard was gunfire...lots of it. Carlson and Woods stared through the broken window and watched the scene frame by frame. Four black SUV's drove up with tires screeching to a halt. It was FBI and ATF. Woods and Carlson joined them, running into the warehouse; Lockett ran with them.

Death had a field day as three Asian men and eight Russians were killed in the gunfire. Carlson was wounded and Lockett...was nowhere around.

The rest of the men were rounded up, cuffed and led to waiting patrol cars. Jergensen was upset on hearing the news of Carlson but somewhat comforted by the fact that his wound wasn't life threatening.

"Woods, who were the Asians? What happened to that guy Lockett?"

Woods' only response was "We couldn't find him Bruce; he just disappeared."

"What do you mean he just disappeared? Wasn't he with you and Carlson? How could he have just disappeared?"

Woods could not answer any of the questions, and therefore refrained from guessing.

#

Chapter 58

When Gregorvsky was told of the hit on his men, he became enraged. "I'm coming back to Philadelphia this evening," he told his next in command on the phone. "Do nothing…I repeat, do nothing with those agents. They can rot in that room for all I care. No one should find them. Understand?"

"No food or water?"

Gregorvsky was adamant. "No nothing."

He paused. "I want Hasai's head on a platter."

#

Ichiro Hasai also heard about the hit. In addition, he learned that the men who carried out the hit were Asian. This complicated matters because he knew *the stubborn- ass Russian* would think he had something to do with the hit. He would take care of Gregorvsky, but right now, he had to find out if the hit had been committed by a splinter group.

#

Chapter 59

Onella Katenta and her men were ready for this new courier coming off a Southwest flight from New York. Her vehicle followed the cab on Interstate 70 all the way to the Westin Philadelphia in the Center City area. *He would soon walk across the Ben Franklin Bridge, just like all the others. And, just like all the others, he will meet his maker too.*

#

Keaton got to the point. "Stanton, my people have Onella Katenta. What do you want to do with her?" he asked.

"Have them hold her for armed robbery, assault, threatening to do bodily harm, whatever Keaton. Let Philly P.D. handle this one. We have to know why she is involved in the killings. I'll be there in the morning so hold off on threatening her life until then. Can you do that?"

Keaton scoffed at Abrams' usual unfair criticism of CIA operations. "Yeah I think we can do that Stanton."

#

Any attempt to interrogate Onella Katenta proved futile. Chief of Police Samuelson and Stanton Abrams waited for an attorney to be appointed for her. She was mute until her attorney arrived.

"You recognize" her attorney began, "you have little to no concrete evidence that my client had anything to do with those courier killings?"

Samuelson spoke first. "Ms. Damon, you can play these games if you want to but we can place your client, through several eyewitness testimonies at the scene of three of the courier murders."

"This is absurd," she said. "Just who are these so-called witnesses Chief? What stake do they have in this? Is there a reward; is this what they want?"

"Ms. Damon, there is no reward that this Agency knows of and for that matter (looking at Stanton) any agency? Three different unrelated eyewitnesses picked your client from a lineup. All we want to do is ask her why she is involved in the courier slayings."

Ms. Damon then whispered in Katenta's ear who said something back to her in her ear. "What will my client gain from this if she helps you?"

Samuelson spoke. "I don't know, maybe instead of life *without* the possibility of parole, we could look at life *with* the possibility of parole. We know that she is not the trigger puller but we do believe she is looking at accessory and conspiracy to murder. She is the brains behind the outfit. Of course we would have to talk to the D.A. first as we are not on the negotiating side of this case. Your client is looking at real time if she does not assist us. Don't get me wrong, she will do time. It's up to her as to the kind of time she wants to do.

Stanton spoke. "She can make it easy on herself and everyone involved if she agrees to tell us who else is caught up in this, why the couriers - and can she deliver Hasai or Gregorvsky. If yes to any or all of these questions we will absolutely work on time with the possibility of parole."

"Okay" Damon said. "I will advise her. First, I must have time with Ms. Katenta and then we will talk with you. Will this work for you *Officers?*"

#

Chapter 60

Tim, Janet and Asgedom's kidnappers returned about an hour later to the darkened room. The urine smell was so pungent that one of the kidnappers had to open a window a little bit so as not to gag.

"You guys stink!" he said. He looked over at his partner and continued with, "don't you think they need a bath?" "No Sergei," the other said. "Remember we were told to leave them alone. They can rot in their stink. Let's just get our stuff and get out of here."

"I think I have a better idea Leonid." With that, he left the room while his partner kept his gun pointed on all three agents. Sergei returned five minutes later with a large container of cold water, which he threw on all three agents. "Can't say we weren't kind. At least now you won't die from the smell."

With that, both men left the room laughing. The agents heard a vehicle drive away. They realized the men had forgotten to close the window.

#

Chapter 61

"Howard, I lost Janet's GPS signal."

"How did that happen, Ahmad? Weren't you just working on their specific location? Didn't you have it 15 minutes ago?"

"Yes Howard, but either the ring got wet or the setting was destroyed."

"How?"

"I don't know."

"Ahmad, let's say it got wet?"

"Howard, if it got wet we have to wait at least an hour before it dries and even then it will might only work only intermittently."

Keaton looked at Ahmad. "I don't want to think about how it might have gotten destroyed."

#

Chapter 62

"Ms. Katenta" attorney Damon said softly. "I would like you to tell the D.A. your story."

"My name is Onella Katenta Samadu. I am from Kabinda, a small village in Democratic Republic of the Congo. My family, although very poor, rubbed together all the money they could to send me to the best school in France. I did not want to leave them but I felt I was their only hope to keep us from begging for the table scraps left us by the foreigners. In my final year at University, I was honored, as well as happy to assist on a project relating to the processing of milk. I was overjoyed at the thought of returning home full of complete knowledge of the dairy industry so that my brothers and sisters would no longer have to work in the diamond mines. I felt that if my family could become agrarians again we would not have to depend on anyone, *especially foreigners* for our food and clothing."

"While in my last year I was given the terrible news that my little brother Peter had died of a heart attack. He was only twelve years old! Twelve years old! The diamond mine owners worked him to death. I could no longer stand by and watch those callous people continually kill our children by working them to death. I decided that I would confiscate diamonds coming into the states no matter how long it took. I believed, and still do, that jewelers would be afraid to purchase diamonds if couriers kept on dying leaving no recourse for the jewelers but to simply disappear. We began in Texas but quickly moved to Philadelphia because the jewelers here are the most arrogant. I never realized the couriers would not give up their inventory, no matter the price. This is how much hold the owners have on little people. The first courier's death was unintentional. The fencing was only supposed to restrain him but he slipped and fell and the metal dug into his neck cutting off an artery."

"What about the subsequent deaths?" the D.A. asked. "Did they slip too?"

"No, they were men who would not let go of their merchandise no matter the cost. I am sorry for them, but I am sorrier for the children of my people."

"Did you know that one of the courier's was an ex-FBI agent? The D.A. asked.

Katenta became quiet. "Not right away; in fact, not

until weeks later. I remember seeing his face in Kabinda several times. I believe they called him Harry."

"How did you know the courier's schedules, when they were coming into the U.S., specifically Philadelphia?"

"My classmate knew several former couriers so I met with them and they supplied me with all the details."

"Would this classmate be Julius Beebo?"

Katenta would not answer any questions about her accomplices. **"Others are on their way,"** she said. **"They will come armed with revenge. My little brother's death will not go unnoticed...not by you or the venomous terrorizers who keep fighting over rocks they call precious. Precious to whom? Not my people. They will come, just like me. This is in no way over. The diamond owners and intermediaries must end their hold over our children and my country. Five deaths for my brother, that is still not enough. Do what you want with me...it does not matter. My brother will not come back from the grave."**

She was led away.

#

When Howard was told of Onella Katenta's arrest, he felt both sorry for the young woman and for her victims and their families. "It didn't need to turn out this way", he said to Jergensen. "I don't care what Stanton said. This conflict diamond business is killing the wrong people. Take it for what it's worth."

Jergensen could not help feeling the same way; in fact, he agreed with Howard. *The people in Africa causing their own children to die at unimaginable rates must be stopped, but in some other way that doesn't include murder.*

No matter how Jergensen looked at it, the woman conspired to have five people murdered. No matter what, she had to account for those men's deaths.

#

"Howard, have we heard from your people yet?" Keaton asked, bringing Howard back to another reality.

"No Rick, we haven't." At that moment Howard's cell phone vibrated – it was Gil Holloway. Howard put him on speaker. "Howard, we have photos of Tim, Janet and Asgedom," he said calmly. "It appears that the back of their car was parked in a way in which we were able to capture some footage of what looked like Asgedom being pushed into a vehicle. When we got to the parking lot Janet and Tim's car wasn't there so one of them had to be an unwitting driver because their vehicle is inoperative to everyone but them."

"Anyway, we ran the plates and found out that the car is a rental. We called the rental company and the owner said the vehicle had been missing for two days but was just recovered a little more than three miles from the jewelry store on Flagler Street."

"On the west side of Miami?" Rick asked.

"Yes Rick," he answered.

"Wow," Howard exclaimed. "That's great work Gil! See if Miami picked up any fingerprints. Look everywhere. Also check for i.d.'s on who rented it and if they used cash."

"They used cash Howard, but the rental company is willing to let us view their in-store cameras to see if we recognize any faces."

#

Chapter 63

"Tim, let's try it again." Tim was trying to crawl on Asgedom's back to try to push out the window screen with his feet. "Ready?" Asgedom asked."

"Yeah" Tim answered. Asgedom bent over slightly as Tim tried to crawl on his back. It was no use; it was too awkward and he was too heavy. Janet was next. As she attempted to crawl on Asgedom's back, it was then that she remembered where she had seen Harry Dennis before.

#

1973

Janet and her friends had been playing softball in the park across the street from her house when she realized she had lost her door key. Her friends helped her search everywhere but they couldn't find the key. There were too many trees and bushes. Her parents were going to be angry once they returned home because this was the second key she *misplaced* in two months.

A thought entered her eleven-year old head. She

remembered that her parents' bedroom window was open. She ran to the garage to get her father's ladder but found the garage door locked. She was desperate. *I could climb on one of my friends back, push the screen in and enter the house!*

Good idea, however, she had to recruit one of the boys to help her. The task took longer than she wanted it to because she had to negotiate with the promise of her newly bought Jackson 5 record. Once she pushed through her parents' bedroom window screen with her fists, she fell to the floor, which sounded like a ton of bricks falling.

"Are you okay Janet?" her friend yelled from outside. "Yes" she answered. "You can go home now."

"No way Janet" he yelled back. "You said you would give me the Jackson 5 record." Janet went across the hall to her bedroom, grabbed the record and noticed her door key on the dresser…where she had left it. She reluctantly threw the record like a Frisbee out the window. "Thanks" he yelled and scampered off.

She tried desperately to put the screen back in the window…with no success. She finally just closed the window.

A metallic glint caught her eye as she was leaving her parents bedroom. She moved in for a closer look. Her mother's dresser drawer was slightly open and a beautiful jewelry box was glistening in the light. It contained two folded up pictures of her mother and a white man she had never seen before. They were young, had their arms around each other, and were smiling.

Janet wondered who the man could be. She had never seen him before but was not about to tell her mother she had found pictures of her and another man while she was snooping in her dresser. She turned the photos over and both read "To Joop from Harry." She wondered who Joop was. She heard noise downstairs; the family was home. Janet carefully and quickly put the jewelry box back where she found it.

The picture took a backseat for 25 years.

#

"Asgedom, I'm slipping" Janet yelled. "Hold still." Asgedom tried to obey her but the combination of his hands cuffed behind his back and all three of them being doused with cold water was too much and he accidentally jerked. Janet slipped and fell on the floor with a heavy thud. She skinned her knees and bit her lip, which made the blood gush quickly from her mouth.

"I'm really sorry Janet," he said. "I'll try to be more careful this time." Janet gave him a look that made him *and* Tim shrink. She tried climbing Asgedom's back again, but still could not maneuver without falling off. A thought hit her like a ton of bricks. She laid on the floor in a fetal position and was able without major difficulty to slip first her butt, then her legs through her arms so that the handcuffs were now in front of her body. She smiled and exhaled. She couldn't believe she hadn't thought of this before now. Tim and Asgedom tried the same maneuver but were unable to complete the same feat. This time Janet climbed on Asgedom's back, pushed the screen out of the window with her fists and rolled out of the window into the sunshine. Since there was no furniture or any type of apparatus in the room the question now on the other two agents' minds was "who will be left in the room?

#

Chapter 64

Ahmad was determined to find the agents. He and Holloway worked on the GPS signal for four hours with no success. He then remembered Dr. Eliot Denny. "Gil, let's contact Dr. Denny and see what he can do to help with this." Holloway was already on his way to their car.

#

Stanton Abrams was beyond pissed when he was told that Tim, Janet and the CIA OPS had been captured. "I told you Forrestal was not ready for lead agent! I said this and none of you listened!"

"Stanton", Howard began, it wasn't Forrestal's mistake. Gregorvsky was smarter than we thought. Besides, Forrestal activated her ring, just like she was supposed to do. Give her credit *please*."

"Do we know where they are?" he asked. Howard did not want to answer the question instead saying, "We have their coordinates and Ahmad and Gil are working on ..."

He cut him off. "So you don't know where they are, or if they're still alive do you?"

"No Stanton, we don't."

#

Chapter 65

Eliot Denny was all too happy to assist the agents in their quest, especially agents for which he and his colleagues had designed a ring. "If someone found the ring" he said, "in a matter of days the sterling silver setting and the silicon carbide in the moissanite would have contaminated each other making the silver soft enough that it would break. If the setting got wet, contamination would set in even sooner, almost immediately causing your recovery system to fail."

"What are we going to do Dr. Denny?" Ahmad asked.

He thought a weighty moment. "What about your car's camera Agent Waverly? Don't I remember you saying you put the same type chip in it?" Ahmad wanted to kiss him; instead, he hugged him vigorously. "If we zone in on the car's chip we can find the car. Hopefully it wasn't abandoned far from Tim and Janet's location."

Before they had an opportunity to check on the car's chip, they were given information about an anonymous call made to the Miami FBI office. The caller had been succinct: "Little Haiti, green house, blue blinds; agent's in back underground room."

Ahmad and Gil drove like bats out of hell until they reached the area of Miami called "Little Haiti." It was appropriately named due to the numerous shacks, trailers and low-income houses owned by...Haitians.

Looking for a green house with blue blinds was almost a joke, as so many houses were green with blue blinds or blue curtains that the agents thought there must have been a major paint sale for these two colors at the local Home Depot...or someone lead them on a wild goose chase.

Gil had been driving for almost 30 minutes when something caught Ahmad's eye. It was someone rolling out of a window onto the grass.

It was Janet.

After Tim, Janet and Asgedom took showers and changed clothing, all the agents on the case met in Stanton Abrams' hotel suite. Woods and Keaton joined the meeting via speakerphone. Asgedom reported first.

"I was in the jewelry store at 0900 hours when Gregorvsky and four of his men came into the shop. Gregorvsky asked if Ms. Davenport and Mr. Hayashi would be coming into the shop. I thought it strange that he would ask this question. I told him I had no idea since Ms. Davenport's ring now fit perfectly. He asked that I contact "the lovely couple" as he wanted to talk more about the quality of her ring and how she felt about it and other, I considered inane, questions. Although my flag was up I still sent Agent Yamamoto a text to come to the store but to converse in Japanese only. Before the agents arrived, Gregorvsky seemed to be looking at other gems in the display cabinets. The two DEA agents were in the store at the time posing as an

engaged couple. They left before any fireworks started because they had no weapons on them, just in case. I presume they contacted DEA.

Keaton said yes.

Asgedom gave more details about their imprisonment. He made sure he left out the graphic and embarrassing details as to why all three of them smelled like urine. When he finished he thanked Ahmad and Gil.

Tim was next.

"I received a text from Agent Asgedom around 08:30 hours. He wanted Agent Forrestal and me to get to the jewelry shop as soon as possible. When we arrived, Agent Asgedom was texting me again requesting us to speak in Japanese only. Gregorvsky took us by surprise."

Tim confirmed Asgedom's account of the day's activities. Before he finished he wanted to make it clear that if it hadn't been for Janet's resourcefulness they might not have been found alive. Janet lowered her head and smiled.

Janet told essentially the same story as Tim and Asgedom.

"After Gregorvsky's men attempted, but could not drive our issued vehicle, Gregorvsky made me drive it with one of his men holding a gun to the back of my neck all the way. I looked in the rear view mirror and noticed that Gregorvsky's men, but not Gregorvsky, were right behind us. I appreciated Ahmad's work knowing that our camera would not only get the license plate of the other vehicle but a picture of both men in the front seat of the SUV.

Because I felt extremely uncomfortable, knowing that I was probably going to die, I almost went through a red light. The man behind me told me that if I made another mistake he would make sure one of my partners was killed."

"After we reached the house, I was lead down a flight of stairs with the same man holding a gun, this time to my back. I was cuffed with mv hands behind me. A few minutes later, I heard Agents Yamamoto and Asgedom's voices. You know the rest of the story."

#

Chapter 66

"What is it that you want Tim?" Kelly asked tiredly.

"I'd like to talk about *us* when I get back to D.C., if that's alright with you Kelly."

"Why? What is it they we haven't said or not said."

"We...I...haven't said that I love you in awhile and I do...love you. If you still want us to make a baby I'm ready."

The silence on the other end of the line was deafening. "Well...why this sudden change in attitude? I mean for the past ten years you haven't wanted a child, why all of a sudden do you want one now Tim?"

"Because I want you in my life forever and if a baby will keep you in my life forever then that's what I want too. I love you Kelly."

"Well I'll think about it Tim and when you get back I'll let you know what my decision is...ok?"

#

Chapter 67

"Mother, who is Harry Dennis?"

Juliana Forrestal was stunned by her daughter's question.

"Who dear?"

"Harry Dennis."

"Um…Juliana almost started stammering.

"He was my father wasn't he Mom?"

Juliana took a deep breath. "Yes he was".

The next thing Juliana heard was the sound of a click.

#

Chapter 68

Julius Beebo was recuperating from four broken ribs, a broken thumb and several cuts on his face. The best part of the recuperation was that he was alive. The worst part was someone was trying to set him up. But who…why? Onella Katenta had not returned his several calls. It was not like her to ignore his calls. He would try again later. First, he needed to call his people.

#

The next morning Beebo was quite saddened by the news of Onella Katenta's arrest. He had been the person instrumental in introducing her to several former diamond couriers from Sierra Leone. For a fee, they explained how couriers were paid and when and how they delivered the inventory. Beebo now felt responsible for her escalated rage. *What can I do to help her?* He suddenly remembered an ally. He sent a text.

"OK nds our hlp. She has bn arestd; mtg stl on at HMC."

When Julius Beebo arrived at the abandoned Greystone, six young men, all from the DRC were there to greet him.

"We want to help Onella", one said in Ibinda language. Beebo answered him in the same language. "That is what we are here for."

Chapter 69

They were at breakfast when Jergensen asked, "Howard, who do you believe called the FBI?" "Who knew of our people's whereabouts?"

"I'm taking a stab at this Bruce. Who was the only person that both Tim and Forrestal reported seeing in the vicinity of the store when they were kidnapped?"

"I believe they said an Asian man was sitting in a car."

"Yes Bruce, but who *is* this Asian man and why do you suppose he helped us out?"

"My question Howard is why do you think it was him that helped us out?"

"I don't know. I just have this sneaking suspicion that it was him. I wonder if Ahmad can tell us if the camera caught him on tape. If so, we need to talk to this possible knight in shining armor".

"If it *was* him Howard, he had to have followed Janet to the house where they were being held. The big question is…why? Do you think he could have been the anonymous caller? How did he know our people were agents? More importantly, what did he gain by helping us? "

"I don't know Bruce. This case is getting stranger by the day. We need to have a conversation with Julius Beebo."

"Why, how will he be able to help?"

"I don't know; I'm working on a plan."

#

Chapter 70

Although the invitation went out to the seventy-six diamond wholesalers in Philadelphia, only twenty met for the meeting at Hasai's manufacturing plant. An assortment of diamonds in black velvet boxes were placed on three round tables also draped in velvet. Although the buyers could pick them up, weigh them and look at them with their jeweler's goggles, an armed guard stood at each table, making sure the stones did not leave the site. Cash was the only accepted form of payment. For some the sparkle was almost mesmerizing. For others, it was just business as usual. Several of the buyers brought hundreds of thousands of dollars in cash with them so they also brought along their own armed guard. Gregorvsky chuckled to himself.

Hasai spoke. "For those of you who are returning patrons you know the quality of our diamonds. For those of you who are new to our system ask your neighbor, he will certainly vouch for our authenticity. Prices are listed in the booklets on the tables. There will be no negotiations. Price includes cut, clarity, color and carat weight of each stone, marked by a corresponding number on box. In addition, price includes certificate of authenticity and country of origination. You have 30 minutes to make a decision. Thank you."

At that moment, ten heavily armed men all with masks on their faces and wearing gloves stormed into the room instantly putting their guns to Gregorvsky and Hasai's heads. The robbers made all of the men, especially the armed ones, to "throw down your weapons on the floor or these two men will instantly die." One armed guard started to shoot and one of the robbers shot the gun out of his hand. The robbers then took all the briefcases, wallets and clothing from all the men except Hasai and Gregorvsky. They made everyone lie on the floor face down. Then the lights went out. When the lights came on again Hasai, Gregorvsky and all of the diamonds were gone.

#

Chapter 71

The six men from Ibinda met Julius Beebo at the Greystone building immediately after their heist. Beebo let them into the basement. "How did it go?" he asked. The oldest smiled. "We are hoping the diamond dealers will believe Mr. Hasai and Mr. Gregorvsky had everything to do with the theft. We taped Hasai and Gregorvsky's mouths, arms and legs and put them in different vehicles. We then dropped them off in different parts of the woods." He lifted his pants leg and grimaced while peeling off the tape that held a bag of diamonds to his leg.

Beebo asked one last question before he paid the men. "Where is the balance of the diamonds? Mr. Hasai expects us to deliver the bounty to him tonight."

The oldest answered again, "The Japs took the other bags."

Mr. Hasai will be pleased," Beebo said through a smile. "Very pleased."

Prior to the meeting at the plant, one more anonymous call had been made, this time to FBI in Philadelphia. Stanton immediately acted on the information. He called Keaton.

The caller was once again succinct. "Illegal diamonds, 9pm, HMC. Door open on north side of building."

Before Jergensen called Woods and other ATF agents, he called DEA. They would all meet at Hasai Manufacturing Company. The complete team of FBI, ATF, DEA and CIA was suited up for what might become a diamond war.

They reached the plant in time to see a black jeep and two panel trucks drive off in the opposite direction. The agents stormed inside HMC to find over 20 men standing in their underwear. Dazed and embarrassed but not injured, all were ready to talk.

"Gentlemen, you have the right to remain silent..." Woods said with a hard-to-keep straight face.

#

Chapter 72

Howard needed to know. "What happened after everyone was taken down to Area 1 Agent Woods?"

"Within minutes Agent Watson, each guy had their attorney here almost before paperwork was finished. Some did not speak a word; not one word."

"I'm sure Gregorvsky and Hasai are now planning on each other's assassination."

#

"So Howard, what do you think?" Who is this mystery caller? Do you suppose it's the Asian guy? Keaton was biting at the bit.

"Rick, I'm working on a theory. So far, a portion of it has emerged as I thought it would. Give me another day. I promise you'll be part of it ok?"

Keaton had no choice. "Okay".

#

Chapter 73

Yoriuko Hasai and his two younger sons met Julius Beebo at Onella Katenta's apartment.

"You have done as you have promised" Hasai's youngest son said to Beebo. "And for this you have garnered our trust."

Beebo smiled. Hasai's youngest son then gave the money and the gems collected from the robbery of the retailers to Beebo. "This is a lot of money. What will you do with it?" he asked.

"After you close the mine in Kabinda we will distribute in equal shares the money from the sale of these gems to all of the people who will lose their jobs. With our contract in place, we will lease the land from you until we pay it off. Right now and thanks to your family, we are able to purchase dairy, farming and construction equipment. With Onella's thesis on milk processing, we will try to start a dairy operation. This money will also purchase men who will not let anyone interfere in our farming efforts. We will name the company "Peter Samadu Agricultural Effort". Onella will be pleased."

Yoriuko Hasai faced Beebo and bowed. He then shook his hand, turned and left the room. His two sons followed behind him.

#

Chapter 74

Minori Hasai, Koriuko's wife was the daughter of a Yakuza mafia member in Japan in the late '50s. Her father was ousted because he offended a mafia head and refused to apologize. He was later found murdered and according to the police, *they had no clues*. Minori, her husband Koriuko and their three young sons had to escape to the U.S. because Minori sensed the Yakuza might come after her husband or sons. Yakuza thought all women were weak so Minori set out to prove them wrong.

The money she brought to the U.S. from Japan was money found in her father's mattress, which she stashed in her undergarments. Five years later, she helped financially with the establishment of her husband's appliance business after his employers were gunned down in the company's garage. Minori made sure her family would always be seen as model citizens, never causing any trouble...always under the radar. This way she felt they would not to be sent back to Japan under any circumstances. Koriuko became an industrial manufacturer and eventually a multi-millionaire.

The problem began when Minori began to see her oldest

son Ichiro starting to act like her father in ways she could not bear to live through again. He had become unpleasant, arrogant, and secretive. She mentioned Ichiro's behavior to her younger sons who in turn had their brother's activities monitored for over three months. She did not mention her worries to her husband nor did she allow her sons to mention them until she had valid proof. However, once her suspicions were validated her younger sons informed their father who in turn notified the company's Board of Directors of Ichiro's illegal undertakings.

When Minori was told about the diamond mine Ichiro had purchased *with the family money,* and that thousands of children had been mutilated and/or died working under horrible conditions, she vowed she would not let her oldest son embarrass or dishonor their name. She would not let Ichiro shame what she and her husband had accomplished in the U.S. Neither she, nor her other children would ever be dragged back to Japan.

If Ichiro wants to disgrace his own name, he will have to do it from his jail cell or from his grave. Her plan would be to have Ichiro and his partners eliminate each other.

#

Julius Beebo and Daisuke Hasai were contemporaries at the same business school for which they both found a thesis in common: Onella Katenta. Beebo wanted to help Katenta out financially if he could, and Hasai wanted to find out more about a diamond mine that his family owned in the Democratic Republic of Congo.

Katenta helped Beebo by giving him all the information he needed for his thesis, which included the sad tales of children being mutilated and dying of heart attacks and exhaustion from working in the diamond mines.

She helped Daisuke Hasai by telling him of the various

accomplices his brother Ichiro had, not only in Kabinda but in Russia too. She also mentioned the FBI agent and the Philadelphia Police Lieutenant who worked in conjunction with his brother. Daisuke's spirit was dampened by this news as Ichiro was until, now, his role model. He thought maybe he should talk to Ichiro and hear his side of the story. He quickly realized he could not do this because he had promised his mother to keep all information to his chest until she said, "let it go". Minori contacted the FBI in Philadelphia. Stanton Abrams set up a meeting with her and Howard Watson. She would not turn back. She would see this through. She would also not shed a tear for a son who would put them all in jeopardy.

"All of my young life my family lived through hell because of my father's lies. The irony is that my name, Minori, means truth and I will live up to it. How can I help you Agent Watson?"

EPILOGUE

Howard, Tim and Ahmad were drinking coffee in Alberto Marino's office while being somewhat forced to watch him read Howard's full report. Also in attendance were Stanton Abrams and Bruce Jergensen. They could all tell when Marino came to parts in the report for which he wasn't happy because each time he would chomp down heavily on his pen.

"Yamamoto could have died. Forrestal could have died. Knox could have died. Carlson could have died!" Yet not one agent had died. Not one. He breathed a sigh of relief. "A fine job."

"So Ichiro Hasai has been arrested for human rights abuses, diamonds illegally traded to fuel war, conspiracy, child slavery, endangerment of minors, what else?"

Howard smiled. "Lots more Al, however let's just go with those because he is looking at 25 years alone for these atrocities."

"And Gregorvsky...I mean Krakevich? What happens to him?"

"Sad to report Al, but Ptor Krakevich hung himself in

his cell last night. Nasty scene. This time I identified the body – it's him alright."

"Bruce, what about Agent Carlson? How is he doing?"

"He'll live. Oh, Al, I almost forgot. Agent Woods said Benny Lockett was found dead of gunshot wounds in the warehouse. Carlson told him in the hospital room that when he was hit Benny had dragged him out of the warehouse. I guess Benny's demons are finally gone. "

"One last thing Howard. Chief of Police Samuelson called and said two lieutenants, one medical examiner and two officers were all brought up on conspiracy, smuggling and weapons charges, and aiding and abetting. *I will bet* several of them will be singing like sopranos." All four men laughed.

Marino rose from his chair. "Okay, everybody, we can probably call this a wrap. I need all your reports by 1600 hours today to submit to the Director. I suppose agents, you should consider taking a couple of weeks off just to get your footing again. No arguments; just go… starting now. I will see you all in exactly two weeks for follow-up. He smiled. "Vacation…is starting now. Stanton, if you and Bruce could hang around a little longer I would appreciate it." Both men nodded affirmatively.

Howard, Tim and Ahmad left the Chief's office heading to their own to finish incomplete paperwork and assemble others to take their places while they were gone.

When Howard and Tim were walking to their cars, Howard asked Tim about Janet. "How is she handling the news that Harry Dennis was her father?"

"Not so good Howard. According to Janet, her mother lied to her all her life making her believe her father had died in Vietnam. It seems her stepfather didn't know the truth either. Lies. Some people can't get away from them. I presume her mother had her reasons."

Howard had one last question. "What's waiting for you?"

Tim wondered too as he got in his car and headed home.

END

CPSIA information can be obtained at www.ICGtesting.com
Printed in the USA
LVOW11s2246090914

403330LV00001B/18/P